Heads I wiN TaiLs you Lose

the misadventures of Willie Plummet

PAUL BUCHANAN
& ROD RANDALL

CPH.
SAINT LOUIS

The Misadventures of Willie Plummet

Cover illustration by John Ward.
Back cover photo by Ira Lippke.
Cover and interior design by Karol Bergdolt.

All Scripture quotations are from the HOLY BIBLE, NEW INTERNATIONAL VERSION®. NIV®. Copyright
© 1973, 1978, 1984 by International Bible Society. Used by permission of Zondervan Publishing
House. All rights reserved.

Copyright © 1999 Rod Randall
Published by Concordia Publishing House
3558 S. Jefferson Avenue, St. Louis, MO 63118-3968
Manufactured in the United States of America

Library of Congress Cataloging-in-Publication Data

Buchanan, Paul, 1959-
    Heads I win, tails you lose / Paul Buchanan & Rod Randall.
        p. cm. — (The misadventures of Willie Plummet)
    Summary: Eighth grader Willie asks for God's forgiveness when he neglects his friends in
order to win a coin collecting contest.
        ISBN 0-570-05477-X
        [1. Coins—Collectors and collecting—Fiction.   2. Contests—Fiction.   3. Friendship—
Fiction.   4. Christian life—Fiction.]
    I. Randall, Rod, 1962-   .   II. Title.   III. Series: Buchanan, Paul, 1959- Misadventures of
Willie Plummet.
PZ7.B87717He   1999
[Fic]—dc21   98-32125
                                                                                              AC

1   2   3   4   5   6   7   8   9   10   08   07   06   05   04   03   02   01   00   99

For Kathy and Darryl Scroggins
and their children,
Kristi, Jenni, Darry, Scotty, Timmy, and Andy

Contents

① Classic Coins

Sam tossed a chocolate coin into my waiting mouth. I swallowed it down in one bite and prepared for more. Talk about the perfect partner for a coin eating contest! Besides being one of my best friends, Sam was the star pitcher for her softball team.

"Keep it up, Sam," I cheered.

Standing five feet away, she lifted another chocolate from the dish. As she stepped forward, she made the perfect underhand toss and landed a second morsel on the back of my tongue. Then another. And another. I clapped and begged for more, like a seal getting fish tossed in its mouth for performing a stupid trick. But did I care? No way. I, Willie Plummet, legendary kid of adventure, had a contest to win.

In recognition of 20 years in business, Classic Coins was having a big celebration. The store's owner, Mr. Speer, sent out special invitations to everyone on his mailing list. He also invited his retail neighbors, which was how I got involved. Classic Coins is next door to Plummet's Hobbies, my family's store.

"You're doing great, Willie." Sam pulled back her blonde hair then grabbed another treat and let it fly. I snatched it out of the air. She picked up the pace. I had hardly gobbled down one chocolate coin before she sent another my way.

Pairs of coin tossers and swallowers lined the length of the store, including Crusher Grubb, the school thug, and one of his friends. My family was also in the act. Mom and Dad were judges. Orville and Amanda, my older sister and brother, struggled as a team. Unfortunately for Orville, Amanda wasn't what you'd call the athletic type.

"Come on, Amanda. You're killing me," Orville grumbled as she bounced a coin off his forehead, leaving another mark. His face looked like it was covered with chocolate pimples.

Amanda looked exasperated. "Can't you catch?"

"Not with my eyebrows," Orville complained.

I wanted to laugh, but feared I'd choke.

"Thirty seconds," Mr. Speer announced. He paced behind the teams in a white button-down shirt and loose red tie, like he always wore. His belly weighed heavily on his grey slacks. The handle of a magnifying glass stuck out of his shirt pocket. The smile on his face spread from ear to ear. I could tell it meant a lot to him to see his customers having so much fun.

Sam tossed coins like an automatic pitching machine. "Willie, chew faster."

I did my best, swallowing what felt like a roll of coins in one gulp. I went as fast as I could. Too fast. Suddenly I got the hiccups. *Hic!* My body heaved and I missed the next coin. "Slow—*hic*—down."

"Do you want to win or not?" Sam replied, letting her competitive spirit show. She pitched me another coin. But the hiccups made me a moving target. The coin bounced off my nose. Another pegged my eye.

"Time!" Mr. Speer called out. He received the tallied scores from Mom, Dad, and the other judges. We all gathered around to hear the results.

"And the winner is ...," Mr. Speer paused for effect. "Willie Plummet and Samantha Stewart with 16 chocolate coins!"

"Yes!" I cheered. "Thank—*hic*—you. Thank you very much. What can I say? Sam's got the big arm and I've got the big mouth."

"No argument here," Mr. Speer laughed. He moved behind the long counter and motioned for us to gather around. "As you all know, I'm a cautious man when it comes to showing off my most valuable coins. But since tonight is such a special occasion, I've decided to bring out a few of my treasures."

We all squeezed in, eager for a peek. Mr. Speer's reputation as a national expert on coin collecting increased the suspense. Stepping into his shop was like entering a museum. Wooden bid boards featured coins for sale from local collectors. Framed enlargements of rare coins decorated the walls. Rows of books on coin collecting lined the shelves. Under the glass counter, the silver coins were so shiny they looked like mirrors. We couldn't imagine what was to come.

Mr. Speer placed a polished wood display box on the counter. We edged closer as he lifted the lid. At first sight of the coins, "oohs" and "aahs" filled the room. Four shimmering coins rested on black velvet.

"I'll start with this one," Mr. Speer began. "It's a 1799 $5.00 gold piece in mint shape. Any idea what it's worth?"

"One thousand," someone said.

"Five thousand," another kid guessed.

"At least seven," Crusher blurted out.

"How about over $10,000," Mr. Speer replied.

"I was closest," Crusher announced. "Does that mean I get the coin?"

Everyone laughed but Crusher.

Mr. Speer directed our attention to the next coin on the velvet. "This is a Spanish gold doubloon from 1764. Pirates killed for a chance to fill their pockets with these. For all we know Black Beard himself once clutched this in his hand."

"I'd like to—*hiccup*—clutch it," I said, reaching out. My dad quickly slapped my fingers.

Mr. Speer went on. "The middle coin is a silver denarius. When Jesus taught the parable of a woman who lost a silver coin, he was referring to one of these. Today it's worth at least $1,000. And last of all is a penny."

"A penny!" I laughed, looking around for the same reaction. All I got was silent disapproval. "I mean, it's a nice penny. It just doesn't seem to—*hiccup*—belong in this group."

Mr. Speer smiled. "This is a 1909-S V.D.B. The letters are the initials of the artist who designed it, Victor David Brenner. Because of the coin's almost uncirculated condition, and the fact that it's so popular with collectors, this old penny is worth nearly $500."

"Five hundred bucks for a penny?" I gagged.

"This penny is my favorite coin in my entire collection, and I'll tell you why. When I was about your age, Willie, I found it in a sand box. At the time I had just gotten into coin collecting. But when I realized what I had and how much it was worth, I was hooked. From then on I collected coins with a dream of one day opening my own store. With 20 years of business behind me, I'd say I've got a lot to be thankful for."

I looked at the penny and back at Mr. Speer. I smiled with him. He had spent his career doing what he loved, and it all began with a penny. Once everyone had admired the coins, Mr. Speer directed us to the final game of the evening.

"Speaking of finding rare coins," he began. "This next game is for the kids." A long trough filled with sand was carried from the back room and placed in the center of the store. He told us to gather around.

"What's going on?" Sam whispered to me.

"That's a good question, young lady," Mr. Speer answered. "The sand has coins in it—pennies, nickels, dimes, quarters, and half-dollars, all similar to the kinds of coins you can find in circulation today. But the buried coins are worth far more than face value."

We all pressed closer to the box and stared at the white sand. Sam stood at my right. Crusher Grubb was a few kids down on my left.

Mr. Speer went on. "The rules are as follows: The first coin you find, you keep. Only one coin per person. Show me what you find, and I'll tell you what it's worth. Whoever comes up with the most valuable coin, gets an 1876 silver dollar."

"Sounds—*hiccup*—awesome," I said.

When Mr. Speer said go, we burrowed through the sand like gophers. Soon kids were pulling up coins like crazy and giving them to Mr. Speer to price. It was down to me and Crusher. I pushed my forearms through the sand. My fingers felt their way like strainers, hoping to feel a coin.

"I got one!" I said.

But Crusher grabbed the same coin at the same time. I wasn't about to let go, but my strength was no match for Crusher's. He yanked the coin, and I came with it. I fell on the trough, knocking it to the ground. Sand slid across the floor. And so did I.

② Where's Felix?

If I were small enough to hide under the sand, I would have. I knew everyone in Classic Coins was glaring at me. My parents were probably too embarrassed to admit I belonged to them. I felt bad, but I couldn't give up. I sifted through the sand on the floor until I grabbed a coin. Rising to my feet, I brushed myself off and apologized. "Sorry about that, Mr. Speer. But it may have—*hic*—been worth it. I found a penny, just like you did."

"Not exactly," he said, surveying the damage. "But I admire your determination."

While we cleaned up the sand, Mr. Speer arranged our coins from most valuable to least. He worked behind the counter with his back to us, so no one knew the results. In the meantime his friends and customers milled about, talking coins and eyeing the countless treasures on display.

I recognized some of the people from town, but others I had never seen before. A few looked wealthy enough to mint their own coins. One guy had a long, gold chain with a monocle at the end. He used it to examine the silver coins. He had white hair and eyebrows. His tan skin looked out of place for this time of year, as if he had used that lotion that darkens your skin without the sun. But if he did, I didn't care. He was the kind of coin expert I could learn from. I introduced myself, and we talked for a few minutes.

"And the winner is," Mr. Speer said, turning around, "Leonard Grubb. His 1936-D quarter is worth $25."

I couldn't believe it. That quarter should have been mine. I searched for my penny in the line-up. It was in the middle of the group, a 1926-D worth $5.

"Cool, I'm on top once again," Crusher said.

"Not yet," Mr. Speer added. "The contest isn't over until this time next month."

"What do you mean?" I asked.

"I thought it would be fun to see who can come up with the most valuable collection of coins in circulation. That means one penny, nickel, dime, quarter, and half-dollar. In a month we'll meet to see whose set is worth the most. There's only one rule: no buying coins—from me or *anyone* else. The contest is based on what you *find*. The winner gets lunch on me and a special display case to hold the coins."

"But what if someone cheats?" a kid asked, glaring at Crusher.

"They could, I guess. But what's the point of spending 10 bucks to buy a rare coin when all you get in return is a lunch worth half that? This is just for fun. Who's in?"

"I am," I said. Everyone else did too.

I began to think of how I could get coins. I'd start with my piggy banks, then move on to Orville's and Amanda's. I'd talk to my friends. Friends? Oh no. Felix! I stuck my hand in my pocket and felt the invitation I was supposed to give him. I couldn't believe it. All the time I was in here having fun, Felix was stranded outside waiting to get in.

I walked to the front window and searched outside. How could I forget Felix? I saw him all day at school. I could have just taken the invitation out of my pocket and handed it to him. I'd be begging for forgiveness on this one.

Sam came over and noticed my look of horror. "What's wrong?"

I explained what happened.

"Don't take it so hard," she told me. "Call him and apologize. He'll understand."

"It's not—*hic*—that easy. He was supposed to spend the night at my house. His parents aren't even home, and he's not supposed to be there either."

"In that case you *should* feel bad," Sam told me. "I would."

"Knock it off, Sam. I—*hiccup*—feel bad enough."

"You sound bad too. You've got to do something about those hiccups."

"In a minute," I said. I asked Mr. Speer if I could use the phone. I dialed Felix's house, hoping he had gone home anyway. No one answered.

I hung up and took a big drink of water. Then I held my breath until I practically passed out. But I still had the hiccups.

"Why me?" I complained. Instead of searching for priceless coins, I'd spend my night looking for my lost friend while my body contorted with hiccups. I asked Sam to tell my parents what happened, and I took off in search of Felix.

I wandered in the video arcade and through the park but didn't find him. Next, I stopped by his house. It made sense that he didn't answer the phone since he wasn't supposed to be there. But he could still be cooped up inside. I knocked, rang the bell, then knocked again. Nothing.

"Felix, are you in there?" I yelled. "I'm sorry about tonight. I just forgot."

"Who are you talking to?" a shrill voice called out.

I turned to see who it was. Mrs. Hamper, Glenfield's nosiest neighbor, stood on her lawn across the street. "The Pattersons are gone for the night. Isn't Felix supposed to stay with you?"

"Yeah, but …" I paused, certain that if I told her what happened, she'd be on the phone to his parents and the rest of the town before my next hiccup. "Um … I thought maybe he—*hiccup*—stopped by here before coming over."

"No one's been here but you," she said, her hands perched on her hips. "Sounds like you've got a bad case of the hiccups."

"They're not too—*hic*—bad."

"Come try a batch of Hamper's helper. It'll fix those hiccups in no time."

I debated for a minute. My hiccups were really annoying me. And Mrs. Hamper was as old as the hills. If anyone had some valuable coins lying around, it would be her. But I had to find Felix. Besides, her recipe was probably like that stuff my dad's mom gave him when he was sick. He said it tasted like gasoline. "Maybe another time. Thanks for the offer."

As I jogged down the street, I tried to figure out where Felix could be. Then it occurred to me to try *my* house. Of course. He had gone to my house to wait. He knows where we keep the extra key. I felt relieved. *He's probably just sitting in the den watching TV*, I thought.

Wrong again. I checked the den, my bedroom, Orville's room, the garage, even the backyard. Felix was nowhere in sight. I tried calling Sam, hoping she would be home by now. She was but hadn't seen Felix either.

"How could such a great night end up so bad," she complained. "First Felix disappears, then I come home to more bad news about my softball team."

"What happened?" I asked. "You guys are doing great."

"It's the fundraising requirements. Every team has a quota to meet to pay for uniforms and other expenses. We're way behind."

"But you have a uniform."

"Yeah, *last* year's. We've barely raised enough to pay the umpires."

"What a drag." I felt bad for her. "Sorry I can't help, but all I can think about is finding Felix." I hung up and headed for the door, determined to search every street in Glenfield if necessary. But I only made it to the front yard when my family came home from the Classic Coins party. "Any sign of Felix?"

"Sorry," Dad said.

"I haven't seen him," Mom added.

Amanda and Orville both shook their heads.

"Well, if he shows up, tell him to stay here. I'll keep looking." I searched alleys, empty lots, the 7-Eleven, and our school. I even stopped by the little league park. Lately, Felix and I had gone to several of Sam's softball games. We'd sit in the bleachers, eat peanuts, and watch her pitch. But the park and bleachers were deserted.

I checked my watch: 10:00 P.M. Not good. Even though we were both eighth graders and liked to stay up late, tomorrow was a school day. If we didn't get to bed soon, we'd be dead tired in the morning and never drag ourselves out of bed.

I didn't want to do it, but I had no choice. I jogged downtown to the police station. The lobby was empty, so I walked as loudly as I could on the tile floor. I figured someone would hear me in the back and come right out. But no one did. Leaning on the long counter, I tried to see through the frosted glass window on the office door. "Hello?" I said. No answer. "Anyone— *hic*—here?"

Silence. *That's weird*, I thought. *Where's the officer on duty?* I searched the length of the counter. At Plummet's Hobbies we had a bell customers could ring for service. That way if Dad was in the back room he could come right out. If a hobby store had one, the police department definitely should.

Grabbing the back of the counter, I pulled myself up and looked around. There it was, a red button, just behind the counter. *It's worth a try*, I thought. I pushed the button.

BRINNNGGG! An alarm wailed. I covered my ears and shielded my face. I thought the windows would shatter. *Now* that's *a service bell*, I thought. An officer burst from the back room, his gun drawn. "Get down! Get down!" he ordered.

I dropped face first on the cold tile, praying he didn't open fire.

Ring Bell for Service

BRINNNGGG! the alarm rang out.

"Put your hands were I can see them!" the officer shouted at me. He came around the counter, pivoting and turning. He moved like a soldier who knew the enemy was out there but wasn't sure where.

Something told me I'd hit the wrong button. I decided to fess up before things got any worse. "It was me," I blurted out. "I'm sorry. I thought the button meant *ring bell for service*."

"You *what*?" the officer growled. He leaned over the counter and turned off the alarm. "That button is only used in cases of emergency. Unless I call them off, every officer in the department will respond."

"In that case, maybe you should call them off."

"You think?" the officer grumbled. Returning to the desk, he got on the radio and announced that it was a false alarm. At least I think that's what he said.

He used code numbers I didn't understand. Although the part about a "crazy red-headed kid" hit home.

The officer motioned for me to approach the counter. The badge on his uniform said Sutton. He was six feet tall and all muscle. His short, dark hair was cut to perfection. "Before we even get to *why* you are here, promise me you'll never hit that button again."

"I prom—*hiccup*—ise."

"What was that?" he growled. "Are you getting smart with me?"

"No. I have the hiccups. I pro—*hic*—mise. I promise."

He watched me for a moment, giving me the stink eye. "What do you need?"

"My friend disappeared." I explained to him what happened with Felix.

"What's your friend look like?" Officer Sutton asked.

"He's a little shorter than me and not as muscular."

The officer repressed a smirk then cleared his throat. "Go on."

"He has brown skin and black hair," I told him. "And he wears glasses."

While Officer Sutton filled out a report, I glanced at the wall behind him. It was covered with SPECIAL BULLETINS. Each featured a suspected criminal. One in particular caught my eye. It was a composite drawing of Jack South, a man wanted for burglary and robbery. He was bald on top, with curly brown hair on the sides. In the middle of his long face, he had a pinched nose that lifted at the end like a ski jump. The poster described him as six feet tall, 180 pounds, and extremely dangerous. I leaned forward. Something about him looked familiar.

The officer noticed me staring. "What is it?"

"Nothing. I just thought maybe I'd seen that guy before." I pointed at the poster of Jack South.

"Any idea where?"

I paused, then shook my head.

"Well, if you see him again, let me know. That guy is bad news."

"Too bad they haven't caught him."

Officer Sutton read over the SPECIAL BULLETIN, then tightened his eyebrows. "He's got a list of crimes a mile long. He's an ex-con too. Strange they haven't picked him up by now."

A new thought entered my mind, and I had to ask. "Will Felix be on a poster like that?"

Sutton chuckled. "No, don't worry. Those are for criminal suspects. Your friend hasn't done anything wrong, which is more than we can say for you." He directed his gaze to the alarm button. "I'll notify the officers on patrol to keep an eye out for Felix. If he turns up, we'll call you. You do the same."

"I will. Thanks for helping. Sorry about the alarm." I made it as far as the door before getting an idea. "In case I need to call from a pay phone, do you have change for a dollar?"

Sutton exhaled while reaching into his pocket. He poked at the change in his palm. "Not exactly. I've got two quarters, three dimes, a nickel and four pennies."

"I'll take it." I handed him a dollar and snatched up the coins as if they were gold doubloons. When I got outside, I stopped under a street light to check the dates. The oldest was 1967. *Bummer*, I thought, *not one collectible in the batch.*

I stood there stewing until I remembered why I was out so late: Felix. I made my way down Main Street to continue my search. The night air felt damp and cold. I knew I needed to get home, but I didn't want to quit looking. Not yet. I passed by Classic Coins, now totally dark. It was hard to imagine that just a few hours ago I was in there having the time of my life.

At Plummet's Hobbies I closed my eyes to say a prayer. I asked God to protect Felix and somehow lead me to him. Opening my eyes, I glanced in the front window. It was just as dark as Classic Coins. Or was it? I pushed my face against the glass. A faint glow leaked from beneath the door to the back room. Was Felix in there? I ran to the back door in the alley. Breathing hard, I stopped and bent down to tie my shoe. I didn't need to, but that was my method for getting the hidden key. The door mat said "Welcome" in giant letters. The letters appeared to be part of the mat and all of them were, except the *c*. It was stuck into the mat with glue. If I pulled hard, it would lift up. Beneath it was a spare key.

I used my fingernails to pull up the *c*. The key was gone. That settled it. I quickly replaced the *c* and pounded on the door. "Felix?"

I heard a chair scooting aside, followed by feet on the floor. The doorknob clicked as if someone had unlocked it. But it didn't turn.

"Felix, are—*hiccup*—you in there?" I asked.

No answer.

I held my breath. After seeing the wanted posters, I felt a little freaked out. What if the person in there *wasn't* Felix? Or what if Felix was a hostage? I stared at the unlocked doorknob. It didn't move.

"Lord, be with me," I prayed, determined to find out who was inside. Grabbing hold, I flung open the door and braced myself for the worst.

Felix sat at the table in the center of the lab. That was the name we gave the back room of the family store. Normally it was where all our experiments and inventions came together. But tonight it was Felix's private hideout. He held his glasses with one hand and his shirt with the other. He wiped the lenses without even looking at me.

"Felix? What are you doing here?" I asked, shocked and relieved at the same time.

"Well, look who's here," he said. He held his glasses to the light then frowned and breathed on a lens. He wiped some more.

"How long have you been here?" I asked, wanting answers.

"Since about 7:00. You didn't want me at the party, so I waited here," Felix told me.

"It's not that I didn't want—*hiccup*—you at the party. I just forgot to give you an invitation."

"Did you forget to give Sam her invitation?" Felix asked, his face tight.

He had me now. But I was too mad over his hide-and-seek stunt to apologize. "Not exactly. Sam was there. For some reason I—*hiccup*—forgot you."

"Don't worry about it. Sitting here, all alone, for *hours*, gave me time to read. I came across some great verses." Felix picked up the Bible that was next to him. "Here's a good one, Proverbs 18:24: 'A man of many companions may come to ruin, but there is a friend who sticks closer than a brother.' Wouldn't that be cool? To have a friend stick closer than a brother."

I didn't answer.

Felix went on. "The first part of Proverbs 27:10 is good too. It says, 'Do not forsake your friend.' Makes sense, huh?"

"Yeah," I mumbled, crossing my arms.

Felix had me but wouldn't let up. "My favorite is John 15:13. It says, 'Greater love has no one than this, that he lay down his life for his friends.' "

"Okay, I'm sorry," I said, holding up my hands. "What about forgiveness? Huh? The Bible says a few things about that too."

"I know," Felix admitted, still refusing to look at me. "I forgive you. No big deal. You just forgot me. That's my outstanding feature: I'm forgettable."

"Normally I don't forget you," I protested. "We do everything together. Remember the time we helped Colonel Pike find his lost gold, or when we went over the falls of Big Niagara at the water park? I didn't forget you then."

"That's true. You practically got me killed, but at least you didn't forget me."

"There you go," I said. We sat there in silence for a while. Finally, I spoke. "You didn't miss much—*hiccup*—at the party. It was OK, but that's all." I told him what happened. "If you want in on the contest, I'm sure Mr. Speer will give you a coin to get started."

"No thanks. I'm not much for numismatics."

"Me either. I just want to collect coins."

Felix sighed. "That's what numismatics is—coin collecting."

"See what I mean. Would a forgettable person use a word like that? That's memorable. Numi ... spastic."

"It's numismatics."

"Whatever. The point is you're unique. What do you say about the contest? It's only five coins. It won't cost you anything, and—*hiccup*—you may get a free lunch out of it."

"I don't need a free lunch. I need a personality, or a big accomplishment that would make people want to be my friend."

"Would you—*hiccup*—stop feeling sorry for yourself?"

"Would you stop hiccuping!" Felix looked at his watch.

"I can't. And they're driving me—*hic*—nuts."

"Every 30 seconds. Have they done that since you got them?"

"I guess. It feels like every five seconds."

"Did you try drinking water?"

"Yes. And I held my breath. It didn't help."

A fiendish grin came over Felix's face. "That's it! I'll discover a cure for hiccups. I'll be famous."

"No offense, but this is starting to sound like when you wanted to discover a comet and have it named after you."

"This is different. Not everyone is into astronomy. But everyone gets the hiccups. And nobody likes them. If I discover a cure, I'll have it made in the shade." Felix raised his index finger. "First everyone at school needs to hear your annoying hiccups. Then, when I cure you, I'll be Mr. Popular. When people get the hiccups, they'll come running to Felix. No one will forget me."

The odds of me having the hiccups the next day were slim, but I didn't want to disappoint Felix. He was too hyped about his big idea. Right now we just needed to get home, the sooner the better. If we hurried, I could still look through my piggy bank before going to bed. Just as I went for the lights I remembered Officer Sutton. I grabbed the phone and dialed the police station.

Officer Sutton was glad to hear the news. "That's a nice piece of detective work. Next time I need to find someone, I'll call you."

"Sounds good to me," I said.

Once we headed out back, Felix gave me the key and I returned it to the mat where it belonged. Then we made our way down the alley and to Main Street. We hadn't gone far when the coin expert with the white hair and monocle drove past. I waved, but he ignored me.

"Who was that?" Felix asked.

"A guy I met at the Classic Coins party."

"Looks like he already forgot you," Felix said, putting his arm on my shoulder. "So tell me, how does it feel?"

The Hiccup Healer

By second period the next day, my hiccups had actually gotten worse. I couldn't believe it. It felt like my throat would turn inside out with each one.

Felix was loving it. "This is so cool. Next time you hiccup, open your mouth so everyone can hear you."

We were in Mrs. McNelly's drama class, listening to her lecture. "Forget it. Mrs. McNelly will have a fit."

"Just do it," Felix urged. "Trust me."

Whenever Felix said that, I got nervous. But I really did want him to cure my hiccups, and not just for him, for me. The stupid things were driving me nuts. Every time I hiccupped it felt like my lungs would pop. I needed a cure, and fast. Then I could get back to my real priority, finding rare coins. Last night's search through my piggy bank was a flop. I didn't find one rare coin.

I decided to let my next hiccup go full force. It had been a few minutes since my last one. I was due for a winner. Relaxing my jaw, I waited for a chance to belt it out. Any second.

HICCUP! My throat erupted.

The 10 rows in front of me turned around. And they weren't happy.

"Not again," a few moaned.

"Give it a rest," my friend Mitch complained.

"I'd like to put him out of his misery," Crusher grumbled.

Mrs. McNelly glared in my direction. "Wilbur, if you need a drink, just ask. But be more discreet next time."

I nodded then whispered to Felix. "Are you happy now?"

"Very," he said, rubbing his hands together. "Now leave the rest to me."

I was on my way to lunch when Sam caught up with me in the hall and handed me a note.

"It's from Felix," she said, then quickly walked away.

I unfolded the piece of white lined paper. It read, *Meet me backstage in the auditorium before you go to the cafeteria.*

I couldn't believe it. How cocky could you get? Felix is so sure he can cure my hiccups, he wants to do it on stage. Did he invite in our drama class to watch? I was tempted to rip up the note and go to the cafeteria instead.

"*HICCUP!*" I sounded off, before slapping my hand over my mouth.

Three seventh-grade girls giggled as they walked by. That did it. Seventh grade girls don't laugh at eighth-grade guys. Crushes, yes. Laughter, no. Stage or no stage, it was time to meet Felix. I practically ran to the auditorium. I pushed open the back door and stepped inside. The door closed behind me before I could find a light switch. It was completely dark. Extending my hands, I carefully wove through the long black curtains that hung from the raised ceiling. *Who turned out the lights?* I wondered.

Bump! I tripped over a stage prop and decided to slow down. "Felix?"

No answer.

I felt my way through the black curtains, getting edgy. My hands started to sweat. "Felix, are you— *hic*—in here?"

Instead of finding Felix, I had discovered the quietest place in the school. I took slow steps, carefully shifting my weight from foot to foot. I pushed through another curtain. Then my hand touched something hairy.

"AAAARRRHHH!" it roared.

"AAAAAHHH!" I wailed, scared half to death. I jumped up a curtain and clung to it like a baby holding a blanket. If I could have, I would have climbed for the ceiling. But all I could do was hang there and scream. "Help me! Help!"

Suddenly, the lights came on. Felix and all my friends sat in the front row of the auditorium laughing hysterically. Some pointed at me. Others wiped their eyes.

Crusher stood beneath me, his face covered with costume fur. I couldn't believe how real it looked. He could have passed for a teenage werewolf. "Owooo," he howled.

I let go of the curtain and dropped to the stage. I felt like lunging at Felix and pulling a werewolf on him.

"Well, did it work?" Felix asked, climbing the stage.

"Did what work?" I fumed.

"Are your hiccups gone? I did a little research. A hiccup is an involuntary contraction of the diaphragm. A sudden reaction could reverse it. In other words, getting scared." Everyone quieted down and stared in my direction.

"I think you cured me." I tipped my head back and opened my mouth. I moved my jaw from side to side. "This is so cool. No more embarrassing sounds. No more stress. No more pain in my—*hiccup*—throat."

"Figures," Crusher muttered. He pulled the fur from his face and stomped through the backstage door. Everyone followed.

Felix just looked at me and shrugged. "Strike one."

A day later I was still mad at Felix and tried to avoid him at lunch. But he squeezed in next to me, holding his tray of food and wearing a nervous smile. Thanks to his phoney-bologna cure, I was the school chicken. It's a wonder Colonel Sanders didn't fry me up for lunch.

After yesterday's failure, I hoped Felix would give up on my hiccups. But that's not what happened. Last night he was in the lab until after the store closed, working on a secret formula. I stood behind the cash register going through piles of change. My fingers turned grey and my eyes grew red, but I didn't find a keeper in the batch.

Pushing my lunch tray aside, I picked over the change from my burger and fries. One of the coins, a 1969-D quarter, had potential. "Check it out," I said, showing it to a few friends who were at the Classic Coins party. Too bad they were more interested in bawking like chickens than looking at a coin. Reluctantly, I showed it to Felix.

He glanced at the coin then looked away. "I think those are pretty common."

"What do you know?" I replied.

Felix shrugged without looking at me. He seemed uneasy, which was probably guilt from his worthless scare remedy. "So how are your hiccups?"

"Practically—*hiccup*—gone," I replied, slapping a hand over my mouth. I slept great last night and woke up cured, but on the way to school my hiccups came back with a vengeance.

"Hang in there," Felix said, patting me on the back. "Hope is on the way."

"Not from you, it's not," I told him. He hadn't said anything about his secret formula and that was fine with me. I got up and went to the vending machine to buy a root beer. That yielded another 40 cents in change. Returning to the table, I gulped down a mouthful then looked over the coins. "Check it out, a 1950-S dime." This time I avoided Felix and showed it to Sam.

"It might be worth a dime or so. Who knows?" she suggested. I could tell she wasn't in the greatest mood either.

"A dime?" I protested. "You're as bad as Felix. What's wrong?"

Sam put down her peanut butter and jelly sandwich. "Our Snack Shack worker at the ball park quit, which means my team's fundraising problems went from bad to worse. The Snack Shack was the one area that brought in money. We need another volunteer—fast."

I thought about the coin collecting contest. "Sorry Sam, but if I'm going to beat Crusher and the others, I've got to look for coins all the time. Maybe Felix can help you."

Felix nodded without looking at me. "Yeah, sure, whatever. Willie, lunch is practically over. Hurry and eat."

"You'll do it?" Sam asked Felix.

"Sure. No problem." Felix sipped his milk, darting his eyes in my direction.

"While you're there you can ask everyone about hiccup cures for Willie," Sam suggested.

I waited to sink my teeth into my burger. "If I still have these hiccups in two days, you can—*hiccup*—take a bat to my head."

Felix's eyes lit up.

"That was a joke," I told him. "What you *can* do is keep tabs on the change tray."

Felix nodded quickly. "Okay, okay. Now hurry up, Willie. Eat your lunch."

I was about to take a bite when Crusher stormed into the cafeteria, terrorizing everyone in his path. That could only mean one thing: The candy bar vending machine had jammed again—with *his* money. Crusher was ravenous and on the rampage. At first I leaned over my burger to hide it from him. Then I got a better idea. If I shared my lunch, maybe he'd stop ripping on me. "Hey Crusher, you want some of my hamburger?"

"What I *want* is my Snickers," he shot back.

"Sorry. All I have is this." I started to lift my plate, but Felix grabbed my wrist.

"What are you doing?" he demanded in a harsh whisper.

"Sharing," I murmured. "Maybe Crusher and his friends will lay off the chicken jokes."

"But it's your lunch. He'll polish it off."

"So? I'll buy some chips and get more change."

I waited for Felix to release my wrist, then I handed the plate to Crusher. He took a big bite, then gave the burger to a few of his friends. When it got back to me, I wolfed down the last bite, trying to look tough.

Felix studied Crusher's expression, then mine with anticipation. In a moment I knew why.

"AAAARGHHH!" Crusher shouted. His friends screamed even louder.

"YEOW!!!!" I gagged, copying them. It felt like I had eaten gunpowder and my tongue was the match. The entire cafeteria stared in our direction. Crusher and his friends ran for the nearest drinking fountain. I grabbed my root beer and gulped it down. But that wasn't enough. I fanned my tongue while running through the cafeteria like a red-headed, fire-breathing dragon. "Out of my way!!!"

With the drinking fountain taken, I went for the bathroom. I pushed through a group of kids and turned down the hall. Slamming into the boys' room, I stuck my face in the white sink. I twisted the corroded knob all the way and let the water pour into my mouth. At first I gulped it down. Then I just let it run over my burning tongue and lips.

Felix poked his head in the door. "Well? Did it work?"

"Did what work?" I sputtered, spraying water all over.

"My potion. A little Tabasco sauce here, some horseradish there. I tried to create a reaction in your throat that would offset the hiccup spasm."

"You want a reaction in my throat? Here's one: You're fired!"

Felix flinched as if I had hit him. "Fired? What kind of gratitude is that? I don't hear any hiccups."

"That's because I don't have a mouth to hiccup with!" As the water poured over my lips and down the drain I watched to make sure my tongue didn't drop with it. I waited for my next hiccup, but it never came. I stood up and looked at my dripping face in the mirror. My skin looked pale and my freckles darker than ever. "Felix, I think you really did it." I kept talking, certain my words would be interrupted. But they weren't. I quickly returned to the sink.

"There you go," Felix said.

I ran a little more cool water over my still-burning tongue. The burning died down and I returned to the hall with Felix. "Don't back out on the Snack Shack," I told him. "Sam's team needs help, and I want you to look for old coins."

"I'll do my best," Felix offered. "But I may still be in hiding from Crusher. Everyone at our table knew I fixed your burger."

"Don't sweat it. Crusher won't find out."

Just then Crusher and his thugs burst from the cafeteria. "You're dead, Patterson!"

"You were saying," Felix said. He took off around the corner, as if his feet were as hot as my tongue.

Candy at Cost

That afternoon I was in Plummet's Hobbies behind the cash register. Dad agreed to let me resume my search for rare coins if I kept an eye on the store while he ran some errands. Felix hid behind the boat model aisle staring at the front door.

"Would you get out of there," I told him. "No one's coming."

"You wanna bet? Crusher and his kind don't just forget. I melted their tongues. They'll never forget."

I picked over a handful of dirty pennies. "Congratulations. You're no longer forgettable. Mission accomplished."

"I'm not popular. I'm notorious. There's a difference."

Before I could say anything else, the door burst open. Felix dropped behind the aisle and hid. The customer nodded when I greeted him, then browsed in the model train section. With his thick handlebar mustache and striped hat, he looked like a train conductor.

Returning my attention to the cash register, I started on the quarters. One had nothing but silver on the edge instead of silver and copper sandwiched together. It had to be worth something. The date said 1955-D. I quickly paged through my book of coin values.

"No way," I gasped. "This quarter's worth $200!"

The customer quickly approached. "What's that?"

"This coin," I said, taking a closer look at the book. Then I realized my mistake. "Oops, it's only worth $2. I didn't see the decimal point. Bummer."

The man's face dropped even more than mine.

"Are you a coin collector too?" I asked.

"Um ... no," he said, forcing a grin before glancing around the store. He had a thin nose and grey hair that bushed below his hat. "I'm strictly a model plane man."

"They're over there," I said, pointing to the wall at the end of the counter.

"Great," he said, drawing his fingers across his mustache. He moved to the plane section and glanced over our selection. "Flying replicas are my specialty. I haven't crashed one yet. Knock on wood." He rapped his knuckles on the wall two times.

"Actually, that's drywall, not wood," Felix informed him.

The guy looked startled. "I didn't know anyone else was in here." He knocked on the wall again. "I guess you're right. That isn't wood, is it?"

"What kind of model planes do you fly?" I asked.

"Um … I have a 1968 Avenger that I really like."

"I've never seen a flying model kit for an Avenger."

"It's custom," he told me.

"Really? You should bring it in and show my dad," I went on. "He makes custom planes."

The man avoided my gaze and pushed his fingers against his mustache. "Yeah, I'll have to do that."

I was about to ask his name when the phone rang. I picked it up.

"Willie, it's Mr. Speer. What's with all the knocking?" he asked. His store was on the other side of the wall. He must have wondered what was happening.

"Oh, it was just a customer," I said, smiling at the guy. "Sorry about that. By the way, I just found a coin worth two dollars. It's a 1955-D quarter."

"Good for you. Why don't you bring it by?"

"I have to keep an eye on things here."

"In that case I'll come there. It's closing time anyway."

"Cool," I said, hanging up. "Mr. Speer is coming here to check out my find."

The customer shot a glance in my direction then at the front door. "Well, thanks for your help. I need to go." He quickly stepped outside and turned in the opposite direction of Classic Coins.

"I think that guy hates coin collecting worse than you," I told Felix.

"I don't hate coin collecting," he said, getting defensive. "It's just not my thing. If you need me, I'll be in the lab formulating a plan to get on Crusher's good side."

"Whatever," I said, thankful that my hiccups were gone and that whatever Felix came up with wouldn't be tried out on me.

When Saturday rolled around, Felix had his first shift at the Snack Shack. The woman who managed it gave him a quick overview of the products and prices. I waited outside, hoping Felix would ask about checking the coin drawer. He did, just as she was about to leave.

"If you find a nickel you want to collect for your friend, just make sure you replace it with a nickel, or whatever. You get the idea." she said, sounding even less interested in coin collecting than Felix.

"Oh, one more thing," Felix added. "What about employee discounts?"

"You can have candy bars at cost while you are working. But that doesn't include your collecting friends."

"What if I buy the candy bars at cost with my own money, but give them away?"

I couldn't believe it. Felix was going to mess everything up for my coin connection.

"I suppose if it's just a few, that's fine. But no discounts for friends."

"Thanks," Felix said.

Once the woman left, I moved from behind the Snack Shack to the service window. "What were you trying to do, ruin everything?"

"No, just cover my bases. Remember, I'm still a wanted man."

Felix was referring to the death burger. Somehow, Felix had managed to avoid Crusher all week, which only made him more ticked off. If the Lord hadn't been looking out for Felix, he never would have survived until Saturday.

"What do you have in mind?" I asked.

Felix straightened the boxes of candy bars. "You'll see."

"Well, it'd better be good," I told him. "Because look who's on the way."

Crusher and his thugs stomped in our direction. As they got closer, Crusher directed his friends to surround the Snack Shack.

"There's no escaping this time, Patterson. We've got you surrounded." Crusher leaned his thick forearms on the counter. It looked like, if he wanted to, he could snap it in two with one karate chop.

"Why would I want to escape?" Felix asked. He sounded nonchalant, but I could see he was petrified.

Crusher flared his nostrils. "You know why. My tongue still has blisters on it."

"That was a mistake. An accident. But to make it up to you, here's a peace offering." Felix slid a king-size Snickers in front of Crusher.

Crusher eyed the treat with suspicion. "How do I know it's not poisoned?"

"Test it," Felix said.

"Guys, come here," Crusher ordered. His friends joined him at the counter. "Keep an eye on Patterson while I try this."

They took that to mean grab Felix by the throat, which they did. I hoped Felix knew what he was doing. If not, I would jump in to his defense. But then we would both look like silly putty when they got through with us.

"Go ahead," Felix gasped, his eyes bulging.

Crusher took a bite of the candy bar. His jaw moved cautiously up and down. "Not bad."

Felix offered candy bars to the thugs who had him by the neck. With Crusher's approval they released Felix and started in on the treats. "Well," Felix choked. "Are we even?"

"Even?" Crusher laughed, licking his fingers. "Not even close." He walked a few steps before turning around. "Next time you won't get off so easy." His thug friends fell in line. They headed for a little league game.

"Way to go, Dude," I said, giving Felix a high five.

"What did he mean *not even close?*" Felix asked, sounding uneasy.

"Don't worry about it," I said. "Crusher's happy for now, which means you can start checking the coins for me."

"I can't wait," Felix grumbled.

I gave him the run-down. "Basically, if it's dated before 1950, set it aside. I'll be back after Sam's game to check on your progress. By the way, where's *my* candy bar?"

"Sorry, Willie," Felix replied. "You heard the lady. No discounts for friends."

Bounty Under the Bleachers

When I got to Sam's game, she was on the mound. Two innings remained. They were ahead 9–4. But Sam was in trouble. She had runners on first and second with no outs. She needed a strikeout bad. Sitting in the bleachers behind home plate, I cheered her on. "Come on, Sam. Show her what you've got!"

Sam wheeled her arm under with the speed of a propeller. The softball shot from her hand.

"Stee ... rike!" the umpire yelled.

"Yeah! That's right," I chanted. The extra support from the bleachers made the difference. Winding up, Sam delivered another strike. Then another. With one away, Sam got to work on the next batter. Now that she had things going her way, I shifted my attention from cheering to coin collecting.

I looked around, desperate to find more coins. I tried to think where people might lose them. Then a thought occurred to me. Change fell from my dad's pockets when he sat down in the car. And we were always finding change in the couch cushions. So why not here? Of course! I could check beneath the bleachers. The splintered wood benches that rose behind home plate were ancient, practically as old as Glenfield itself. I looked through the wood boards to the ground. I couldn't see anything, but there had to be a gold mine down there. It made sense.

I casually stepped from the bleachers and wandered to the dirt beneath the seats. I didn't want to attract too much attention to my brilliant plan. The competition would flock to get a piece of the action. At least that's what I thought. But there wasn't a coin in sight. Someone had beaten me to the punch. I was about to leave when an amazing thing happened. A penny dropped on my head. I quickly checked the date. It was a 1987, worth no more than a penny. But I didn't care. I was on to something, something big. And I knew just what to do. Returning to my seat, I waited for the right moment.

"Stee ... rike!" the umpire shouted. He held up his fingers to indicate a full count. With bases loaded, my timing couldn't have been better.

"Go A's!" I chanted. To punctuate my point, I stood up and flung my hands in the air. The people near me took notice.

"The wave?" a woman asked.

I nodded with enthusiasm. "The pitcher's a crowd pleaser. She'll eat it up."

I sat down, then repeated the wave. A few people followed my lead. Soon everyone in the bleachers knew what we were doing.

"Again!" I started us off. The woman next to me followed on cue, along with the rest of the spectators. We looked like an ocean swell rolling for the beach.

Sam glanced our way before releasing her pitch.

"Ball," the umpire said. "Take your base."

I couldn't believe it. After all that, Sam walked her. Some gratitude. Oh well, coins were probably falling like rain. I'd need a wheelbarrow to cart them off.

"Come on, Sam," I shouted, knowing she needed my support now more than ever. "You can do it. Turn it up a notch." Determined to practice what I preached, I turned up the wave machine. I stood and flung my hands in the air, then quickly dropped to the bench to repeat the process. Everyone did their best to keep up. We cranked out enough waves to drown a whale.

If only Sam could show a little appreciation. She threw a ball, then another. The batter couldn't have hit the pitch if her life depended on it. But I wouldn't give up. I moved up and down like a jackhammer. Soon the crowd lost the flow. We looked more like raging rapids than a wave, which didn't help Sam one bit. Her next pitch was so wild it launched straight for my head. Good thing the backstop was there. The catcher got to it and tagged out the girl who tried to steal home. That meant two outs with one to go.

Time to check my bounty. I squeezed between the wood slats and dropped straight down. Sure enough, coins covered the dirt. A dozen at least. Jackpot! I crawled around, picking them up. Above me the bleachers creaked as spectators stood and sat, trying to revive the wave. Unfortunately, the movement had an unexpected side effect.

"Hey!" I gasped. Someone knocked over a cup of soda that poured on my head. It must have been one of those Super-Mega Gulps. It felt like I was crawling under a brown waterfall. I moved aside, but it didn't help. As I reached for a dime, sweet tarts fell like hail. An open packet of mustard came next, followed by blue syrup from a snow cone. I felt like a duck in a shooting gallery. By the time I escaped, my hair was cotton candy. A rainbow of stains covered my white T-shirt.

"Why me?" I muttered. But when I checked my coins, I decided it was worth it. One of them, a 1953 50¢ piece, had to be a winner. I pulled it close to examine the details. It was in great condition. The hair above Franklin's shoulders was still well defined. The letters that spelled "IN GOD WE TRUST" were raised and sharp.

I tilted it to let the sun bring out the details. "Awesome," I said to myself.

WHACK! From out of nowhere a softball hit my hand, knocking loose the 50¢ piece. I looked around, confused. Sam stood in the dugout, glaring at me.

"No!" I cried. I frantically searched the grass, but couldn't find the coin.

"Willie!" Sam ordered through clenched teeth. "Get over here."

I shook my head and dropped to my knees. I had to find the Franklin. I combed my fingers through the green blades. My face hovered just inches away.

"Willie," Sam repeated.

I ignored her and kept searching. But it was no use. I couldn't find it. When I got to Sam I clutched the chain link fence, ready to chew her out. But she beat me to it.

"What were you thinking?" she blurted out. "The wave? You cost us three runs."

"Me? I did everything I could to *help* you. Why do you think I did it?"

"I know why. So you could *steal* money. Your trick was just a tad bit distracting."

"That's the thanks I get?" I complained. I hadn't thought of it as stealing but, thanks to Sam, now I felt guilty. And besides that, other than a head full of sticky cola topped with Sweet Tarts, I had nothing to show for my great idea.

Sam wasn't through with me. "Next time you want to pick people's pockets, don't do it at my game."

"If that's the way you feel, don't worry. I won't come back." I stomped straight for the Snack Shack, burning. A breeze kicked up, but my clump of cotton candy hair didn't budge. My hand throbbed from getting nailed by the softball.

"What's your problem?" Felix asked, noticing my scowl.

I told him what happened, finishing with, "I'm outta here. With friends like that, who needs enemies?"

"Suit yourself," Felix said. "I'll just put the coin I found you back in the drawer."

"Coin?" I said, stopping on my heels. "What coin?"

"Forget it," Felix went on. "We're only here because of Sam. You wouldn't want a coin that has anything to do with her. If Sam's a part of it, you don't want it."

"I don't?" I asked. "I mean … you're right. I don't."

"No way," Felix taunted. "Who cares what it's worth?"

"Worth?" I mumbled, thinking I had taken the mad-at-Sam thing a little too far. "Um … what's the coin anyway? Just out of curiosity, I mean."

"A nickel with a buffalo on the back. I don't remember the date." Felix pulled the coin from his pocket and looked it over.

"A buffalo nickel?" I choked. "Let me see it!"

"Sorry. You're too mad at Sam to even care about this thing."

"I'm not *that* mad. Sam's one of my best friends. We get mad at each other. Then we get over it. That's what friends do. No big deal." I lunged at Felix to get the coin, but he clenched his fist and held it away.

"Will you work things out with Sam?"

"Yes, yes!" I conceded.

He placed the nickel in my hand. It was a 1931-S buffalo nickel in fine shape. I pulled the coin close to look it over, thinking things had finally gone my way. Or so I thought.

"Plummet?" a deep voice questioned. Officer Sutton stood at the Snack Shack window, staring me down. All I could think about was my wave fiasco on the bleachers. Sam had accused me of stealing. She must have turned me in.

The Detail Dweeb

I stared at Officer Sutton, not knowing what to say. My heart pounded. "Um … Yeah. Hi," I finally sputtered.

"What do you have there?" Sutton asked.

"A buffalo nickel. Felix gave it to me."

"Mind if I see it?" Sutton extended his hand. I handed him the nickel. "Looks like a beauty. That ought to help you in the Classic Coins contest." He offered a grin.

"How'd you hear about that?" I asked, relaxing.

"I bumped into Mr. Speer earlier today. He mentioned the anniversary celebration and the contest for you kids." Sutton looked around the Snack Shack. "Anyway, when I saw you come in here, I decided to follow up on our conversation the other night."

"You mean about the alarm?" I asked, getting worried.

"No. Until now, I'd forgotten all about that."

Me and my big mouth.

"I was referring to Jack South, the guy on the wanted bulletin who looked familiar to you. Have you seen him?"

"Not at all," I said with a shrug. "Why? Has he robbed someone else?"

"Not quite," Sutton explained. "But there was a burglary at Ashland Hardware involving several power tools. A witness reported seeing a man similar to the one you noticed in the police station. You can't think of anyone suspicious hanging out near your store?"

"No. We've had a few new customers that I didn't recognize, but they didn't look like the guy in the picture."

Officer Sutton took out a copy of the SPECIAL BULLETIN. "Well, if you see anyone that matches this guy, give me a call at the station."

Felix joined me in looking over the sheet. "Wait a minute. This isn't the guy I first saw on the wall."

"I know. Based on the witness's description, we updated the composite drawing. Notice the added details?"

"Definitely. His nose isn't turned up quite so much, and there's a cleft in his chin. I'll keep a look out," I promised. Suddenly hunting for old coins didn't seem so exciting. Not when I could be hunting crooks instead. As Sutton walked away, I stood in a daze, dreaming of going undercover to catch a thief.

On the way home from the ballpark, I decided to check in at Classic Coins. I wanted Mr. Speer's opinion of the buffalo nickel.

"I'd say that's a keeper," he said enthusiastically. He removed his magnifying glass from the pocket of his white shirt. "I'd grade this fine. The edges of the legs are raised and crisp. It's a beauty all right."

"Can I see it through that?"

"You bet. It's your collectible." Mr. Speer handed me the magnifying glass and showed me the details to look for. "Whether you agree with it or not, collectors want coins that are in mint shape. A little wear on the surface can change a coin's value dramatically."

"But this nickel is hardly worn, and you said it was only fine. Why not extremely fine, or mint?"

Mr. Speer removed a buffalo nickel from under his glass counter and placed it on a piece of black velvet. "May I?" He placed my coin next to his. "You tell me which coin is in better shape, and why."

Using the magnifying glass I went back and forth between the two. "Yours. The buffalo's pelt has more hair. The letters look sharper too."

"Exactly. Coin collecting is all about details. Observing minute characteristics is critical." Mr. Speer pulled out a few more coins and pointed out distinctive features that made each a mint condition coin. "You think you got it?"

I nodded.

"OK. Turn around, and we'll see how you do."

I cooperated and, after a minute or so, Mr. Speer told me to turn back around. Three pennies on black velvet greeted me. "I don't get it."

"Your test is to arrange those pennies from best to worst."

"Is this a joke?" I asked. The pennies looked like they had just arrived from the mint.

"No, sir. You can do it. Remember, details."

Using the magnifying glass, I examined the pennies. They still looked the same. Mr. Speer made his way to the front window and looked outside. He had been checking the window ever since I arrived.

"Ready," I said after arranging the pennies.

"Let's see how you did." Mr. Speer returned from the window. "Not bad. You got the one in best condition right. But you reversed the other two. See this ear? See the edges? They've been rubbed down just a little bit."

Mr. Speer gave me a few more challenges. Little by little, I improved. While I studied the coins, he watched the cars passing by on Main Street. After arranging the last coins, I joined him. That's when I saw the guy from the wanted poster. "That's him!" I blurted. "Jack South! He's wanted by the police!"

Mr. Speer jumped. "Where? Where?"

"Over there!" I said, pointing. "Across the street!"

Mr. Speer looked carefully. "That's Mr. Keefer, your science teacher."

"No, it's not," I said. But I realized Mr. Speer was right. I tried to make light of it. "Well, he's dangerous too. You should see him with sulfuric acid and a test tube. Don't let him near your coins."

"I'll keep that in mind," Mr. Speer laughed. "But Mr. Keefer is no crook. You need a break from that magnifying glass. You're getting nearsighted. Tell me something, since when are you so worried about catching a criminal?"

I explained what happened in the police station and my conversations with Officer Sutton. "He said he spoke with you."

Mr. Speer crossed his arms. "I'm not going to lie to you, Willie. There were a few people at my anniversary celebration that I didn't recognize."

"Do you think someone is planning to break in here, like Jack South?"

"I don't know," Mr. Speer admitted. "But I'm keeping a close eye on all suspicious characters." Just then Crusher entered the store.

I put my nickel in my pocket. "In that case you ought to keep an eye on him."

"Hi, Leonard," Mr. Speer said. "How's the search coming?"

"Excellent." He placed a 50¢ piece on the counter.

"Would you look at that?" Mr. Speer marvelled.

"Sweet, huh? I found it in the grass at the ballpark."

I wanted to cry. "It wasn't near one of the softball dugouts was it?"

"Yep. What kind of stooge would let go of a beauty like this?" Crusher laughed and slapped me on the back. "Did that cure your hiccups?"

"I lost them days ago, along with my taste buds, thanks to Felix."

"That's right; I forgot about Patterson," Crusher said, snapping his fingers. "Where is he?"

"I haven't seen him since I left the Snack Shack."

"Well, if you do, tell him I'm looking for him," Crusher told me.

Mr. Speer placed the coin back in Crusher's hand. "That's worth at least $7. Combined with your quarter from the first night, you're practically untouchable."

"As always," Crusher said, heading for the door.

"Where's Sutton when I need him?" I mumbled. "He should arrest Crusher for public nuisance."

"Don't get discouraged, Willie," Mr. Speer said, returning to the front window. "Just keep at it. You never know what treasure you'll find in your next handful of change."

After church on Sunday, I sat in the den. Amanda had agreed to let me go through her piggy bank. When she turned 18, she opened a savings account, but never got around to rolling the coins. I told her I'd roll them for her if she'd let me have two coins of my choice, regardless of what they were worth.

"This one has potential," I said.

Orville looked up from the football game he was watching. "Really?"

"Yeah. It's a 1968 quarter. Too bad the condition is so poor; it might really be worth something."

"What do you mean?" Dad said. "It looks great."

"Sorry, Dad. Look at the details." I was eager to show off everything Mr. Speer had taught me. "Notice the worn lips and the flat hair. It must have spent the night on a train track. Look how shallow the facial features are."

Dad looked at Orville. "Now that's an eye for detail. I'm impressed. Willie, you are really talented."

"Did I hear someone describe Willie as talented?" Amanda asked, appearing from down the hall.

Orville tossed a pillow at my head. "He's no better at noticing stuff than the rest of us."

"Oh yeah?" I said, eyeing my brother. I'd probably regret it later, but I decided to shift my eye for detail from coin faces to my family's faces. "Here's proof that I've developed a keen eye—the green speck of food stuck in your teeth isn't lettuce from lunch, it's spinach from two nights ago."

Orville scraped his teeth with his fingernail then ate the leftover. "You're right." He raised his eyebrows as if to say, *not bad*. I didn't know if he meant me or the spinach.

"Gross," Amanda said.

"Maybe this newfound talent isn't such a good thing," Mom said. She glared at my dad as if to say, *Make Willie stop*.

But Dad was getting a kick out of it. "What about me, Son? Any details I've overlooked?"

I rubbed my chin. "Well, let's see."

Dad straightened, as if posing for a photographer.

"Your ear hairs could use a trim, either that or a good shampoo. They're out of control."

"Double gross," Amanda said.

"I tried to warn you," Mom reminded them over crossed arms.

"He's just kidding, Dear," Dad told her. "I'm sure your details are perfect."

I tilted my head. "Don't be so sure. Mom may trim her eyebrows, but they still don't match. And her makeup has swirl marks in it, like she frosted a cake."

Mom squinted in my direction. "Oh, I'm frosted all right."

"Mom, quit being so serious," Amanda giggled, having fun. "Your makeup did look a little thick today. No offense."

Mom lifted a lopsided eyebrow at Amanda. "Willie, we're all impressed. Now why don't you get back to your coins."

"But Amanda hasn't had her turn," Orville said.

When I focused on Amanda she winked and flashed a beauty-queen smile. With her strawberry blonde hair and delicate face, she probably felt safe. And if I was smart, I would have kept my mouth shut.

8

Pager Problems

Hesitantly I studied Amanda's radiant features. I hadn't forgotten whose coins I was rolling. "I can't see much."

"Chicken," Orville chided. He tucked his thumbs in his arm pits and flapped his elbows. "Willie can be bought. Bawk ba-bawk."

"Yeah, right." I shrugged it off. But he kept at it. I was sick of being called a chicken. I had to save face. "Okay, maybe her right nostril is larger than the left. There. I said it. Big deal."

"Her nostrils?" Orville complained. He flapped some more. "That's obvious from a mile away. You're no expert on details."

"All right," I said, ready to put him in his place. "She used extra blush to hide the pimple on her chin."

Amanda held her hand over her mouth. "Is it that obvious?"

"I've seen less clay on a potter's wheel," I joked.

"Not bad," Orville admitted.

"That's nothing," I went on. "Look at her eyeliner. It's clumped together like tar. And her bangs look like they were attacked by a weed whacker."

Amanda grabbed my collar. "You little brat. That's the thanks I get?"

"What? I didn't even say anything about your lip fuzz."

Orville stopped flapping his wings. "This is getting good."

"Maybe you'd like to eat these coins," Amanda said, grabbing a handful.

"I tried to warn you kids," Mom said. "But you wouldn't listen."

"Did you?" Dad teased. "I couldn't hear you. My ears are full of hair."

"And Amanda's ears are too small," Orville added, trying his hand at observation. "They belong on a chipmunk."

"Now I have chipmunk ears?" Amanda growled. She tightened her grip.

"Orville said it, not me," I gasped.

"But you started this mess." She pinned me on the couch with her knee on my chest. "Say your prayers, Detail Dweeb."

If it wasn't for the doorbell, I might have been a goner. Amanda jumped off me and straightened her hair. Moving to a chair, she sat upright and crossed her legs. She'd die if a visitor saw her in anything other than a ladylike pose, especially a guy. Dad went to the front door and came back with Sam. Her shoulders dropped over what looked like a 20-pound box.

"What's wrong, Sam?" Orville asked.

"Yeah, did Willie detail you too?" Amanda followed.

Sam slumped onto the couch next to me. "Another rejection and I quit. I've been trying to sell candy for my softball team. I go door to door, explaining who I am and what I'm doing. I beg, I plead. But no one seems to care."

I patted Sam's shoulder. "That's door-to-door sales for you. It's brutal, especially alone. You need someone on the team to go with you."

"That's not a bad idea," Dad added. "But it doesn't have to be someone on the team, just someone to help carry the box and share in the rejection."

Everyone glared in my direction. "I'm too busy looking for rare coins. I don't have time."

"Don't be so selfish," Orville said. He threw another pillow at me. "Besides, there're a lot more coins out there than in here. Amanda's coins aren't going anywhere."

Mom jumped in. "How much does a box sell for?"

"Three dollars," Sam said.

Amanda jumped in. "Tell your customers they can pay in change. People love to get rid of coins."

With everyone looking at me, I had no choice. I was still mad at Sam for what she did at the ballpark, but I decided to help her. I thought of the verse Felix read from John about laying down your life for a friend. Selling candy with Sam wasn't even close to that kind of sacrifice. I agreed to go with Sam on Monday after school. It would be good for our friendship and maybe I would even find a rare coin on the way.

Arriving late to drama class, I hurried to get to my seat. I sat down behind Felix just as the bell rang.

"I can't believe you," he started off. "You did it again."

"Did what again?" I asked.

"You blew me off. When Crusher found me yesterday, he practically killed me."

Suddenly I remembered not telling Felix that Crusher was looking for him.

"Oops," I said quietly. That explained why Felix didn't return my call after church. We had planned to hang out, but he never got back to me. "Sorry about that."

"I barely got away alive. Good thing I had something to bargain with other than my blood. I also figured out a way to get by without flaky friends like you."

"Good for you," I said, feeling discouraged. Then I realized I had just admitted to being flaky.

Felix reached in his pocket and produced a pager. It was black with a digital readout on one end. "If anyone wants me, I'm only a phone call away."

"You got your own pager? Cool, let me see it." I grabbed for the pager, but Felix held it at arm's distance.

"Sorry. You might forget who it belongs to and not give it back. Besides, I'm waiting for an important call."

Mrs. McNelly, our drama teacher, clapped her hands. "Quiet down, class." She quickly took roll, then turned her attention to Crusher sitting in the back row. "I believe it's your turn today, Leonard."

Crusher stood up and eased to the front. His fingers tapped nervously on each desk as he navigated the row. Every student watched with anticipation, even awe. He had total stagefright. Everyone in class had to perform a two-minute soliloquy. That meant standing alone in front of 35 students and acting out part of a scene from a play. You couldn't look at the script either. And if you messed up, you had to start over.

Crusher picked a character from *Our Town*. He cleared his throat and stared at his feet. "This time nine years have gone by, friends ..." He glanced at the audience, then returned to the safety of his feet. When he was almost done he made eye contact with Mrs. McNelly. She nodded with approval. Finding his place, Crusher raised his voice to finish strong. Everyone leaned forward, ready for the big ending. "What's left when memory's gone, and—"

Beep! Beep! Beep! Felix's pager went off. It sounded like a car alarm. Everyone twisted and turned until they found out the sound was coming from Felix. *Beep! Beep! Beep!* He fumbled with the pager, pushing every button on it. Finally, it shut off. Felix didn't bother with the number on the readout. He just shoved the pager in his pocket.

"Now you know why some schools have banned those things," Mrs. McNelly said, frowning at Felix.

"Sorry," Felix whispered.

When we returned our attention to the front, I expected to see smoke pouring from Crusher's ears. But he just stood with loose arms and a queasy expression, like he was facing a firing squad.

"Under the circumstances, you can pick up where you left off, Leonard. There's no need to start over," Mrs. McNelly explained. She motioned toward Crusher. "Continue."

"Um ..." Crusher started. After bumbling a few words, he stopped. "I'm blank."

"If you lost your flow, you'll need to begin again. And this time address your audience, not your feet. We're ready when you are." She clapped her hands.

Felix was the only guy in the room more petrified than Crusher. He slid down in his seat.

"This isn't fair. Felix made me lose my place," Crusher protested.

"A good actor can overcome distractions," Mrs. McNelly explained. "Glance at your lines, then begin again."

With a trembling hand, Crusher picked up the book. His eyes raced across the page. Once he got going, he made it, barely. At one point, Mrs. McNelly had to coach him. We all breathed a sigh of relief when Crusher walked to his seat. He went out of his way to step on Felix's foot as he passed.

After several more students took their turn, the bell rang. I knew I'd regret it later, but I decided to stand in the aisle in front of Crusher. I wanted to give Felix a head start so he could get away.

He did his best, weaving past desks and students for the door. Crusher stalled behind me for a moment then figured out what was happening. He tossed me aside. The desks I landed on scattered like bowling pins.

When I got up, I chased after Crusher, wanting to help Felix. I found them in the hall. Felix was pressed halfway into an open locker, his throat hidden behind Crusher's thick hand.

"I ... ga ..." Felix sputtered.

"Crusher, let go," I said, feeling brave for Felix's sake. "He's trying to tell you something." Crusher eased up.

"I got it," Felix gasped.

"Got what?" Crusher demanded.

"Your candy bar order." Felix told Crusher that he would pick up the candy bars in the afternoon and bring them to school in the morning. He also told him the price.

"That's pretty good," Crusher said. "That's why your pager went off?"

"Yep. I told them to page me if your order was approved."

Crusher put Felix down and let go of him.

"If you ever need to get ahold of me, don't rely on forgetful people," Felix said, glancing in my direction. "Just page me." He wrote out his number on a piece of paper.

"All right," Crusher said, still cautious. He looked at the number on the paper then put it in his pocket. "Tomorrow morning then. Find me."

Felix straightened his shirt as Crusher and his friends walked away.

"What was that all about?" I asked.

"That's why Crusher wanted me the other day," Felix explained. "He's got a sweet tooth. I talked to the lady who runs the Snack Shack about selling candy at a discount when I'm away from the ballpark. She said it was fine with her, but she'd have to check with the league."

"I don't believe it," I said.

"Believe it. It's a win-win setup. The league raises even more money, and I'm suddenly Mr. Popular." Felix tossed his pager in the air, caught it, then plopped it in his pocket. Slinging his backpack over his shoulder, he strutted down the hall. I just stood there with a dopey expression, feeling useless.

⑨

Felix Goes Hollywood

The house in front of us looked like a castle. The walls were made of black stone. In the courtyard a small waterfall poured into a fish pond. Purple flowers dangled over the sides of hanging pots.

"Talk about *Lifestyles of the Rich and Famous!*" Sam said. She touched the doorbell and we listened to it chime.

"I'll bet this place has coins from the middle ages," I whispered. Grabbing Sam's arm, I positioned her in front of me. "You'll make the best first impression." Earlier in the day, I had told Sam to wear her uniform when we went door to door. I thought it would help sales. At first she objected, saying her mom would freak out if something happened to it, especially since it was worn out already. But when she came to my house after school she had it on. She had even borrowed a coach's jacket for me.

"We're not here for the coins," Sam reminded me. "So don't be a pest."

"But I'm on a hot streak." At the last house the woman paid with a 1932 quarter. A quick check in my *Pocket Coin Guide* revealed it was worth $6.50. I lifted Sam off the ground like we had just won the World Series.

"Since when is one quarter a hot streak?" Sam rang twice and we waited.

"What was that?" I asked. It sounded like shoes on tile moved behind the door. When no one answered, Sam rang again.

"How weird," I said, sliding between Sam and the door. "Here, give me a boost."

"No way."

"Come on," I reasoned. "I just want to see if someone is in there. If not, we'll leave." After more persuasion, Sam boosted me to the small window above the door. The foyer looked like a museum. A white sculpture of a guy's head rested on a pedestal. The floor was black marble. A chandelier hung from the vaulted ceiling. Gold-framed paintings decorated the walls. But there wasn't a person in sight.

"Hurry, Willie," Sam grunted. She wobbled, and I almost lost my balance. That was enough for me.

"Put me—" I stopped mid-sentence. A man wearing socks rushed into the foyer from the hall. He eyed the paintings for a moment, then removed one from the wall. It took a minute for his face to register, but then I knew who he was—Jack South from the wanted poster.

"Down! Now!" I hissed, trying to whisper and shout at the same time.

The man glanced in my direction, then disappeared down the hall.

"Quick! Get out of here!" I pushed Sam backwards to get her going. But instead she stumbled into the fish pond, seat first. Reaching down, I grabbed Sam's hand and backed away from the pond. She dragged on her belly over dirt and flowers before climbing to her feet. "Run!" I ordered.

Sam followed me across the lawn to the house next door. I rang the bell and pounded, desperate to use a phone. No one answered. We couldn't risk trying another house. What if Jack South caught us? A dead witness is a silent witness. We had to get out of there. We sprinted to the end of the block. Across the street we found what we needed—a pay phone. Stuffing my hand in my pocket, I found a quarter and dropped it in the slot. I dialed the police station and asked for officer Sutton.

"I found the guy wanted for robbery," I blurted.

"Who is this and what are you talking about?" Sutton asked.

"Willie Plummet. I found the suspect! He's robbing a house." I gave Sutton our location. He told us to stay put. We moved away from the phone enough to keep an eye on the house, just in case the thief tried to escape. In the meantime, I noticed Sam's uniform. It was a sight to behold, black as tar and smeared with pink flowers.

Sam stared down at herself in horror. "Willie, if that guy isn't—"

"The police!" I blurted out.

Sutton arrived with two other squad cars. One headed for the alley behind the house. Another parked across the street. Sutton pulled up next door. While he crossed the lawn, officers took up positions on both sides of the house. With everyone ready, Sutton approached the door. Sam and I crossed the street to get a closer look at the action.

We could hear Sutton knocking. A few minutes later we heard talking. No gun shots or doors breaking down. Just talking.

"They're already reading South his rights?" I asked in awe. "That was smooth."

"Maybe not," Sam suggested.

I was about to object when Sutton walked empty-handed to the squad car. He reached in the open window and pulled out the radio handset. The other officers joined him. They spoke for a few minutes then left in the other cars. That's when Sutton noticed us. We cautiously shifted down the sidewalk in his direction. I flashed a thumbs up, but he responded with a thumbs down. When I got to him I found out why.

"That was the owner of the house you saw."

"The owner?" I asked.

"He was redecorating and didn't have time for solicitors. That's why he ignored the bell. When he saw you looking in the window, he thought *you* were a burglar. He called the station after we left."

"So I called on him, and he called on me?" I said in surprise. "That's funny."

"Funny?" Sutton grumbled. He wiped his forehead, then removed a clipboard and began filling out a form. "From our standpoint we got two calls reporting a burglary at this address. There was nothing funny about it. I know you meant well, but next time don't jump to conclusions."

"Yeah, Willie," Sam said, sinking an elbow in my gut.

Sutton gestured to Sam's uniform with his pen. "What happened to you?"

"That would be Willie's fault. He pushed me in the pond then dragged me out. He was in a big hurry."

"What are friends for?" Sutton chuckled. He hopped in the squad car and turned the ignition. "Remember what I said. Next time, get a closer look."

Once Sutton drove away, Sam was on me like the mud on her uniform. "Look what you did! My mom's going to go berserk. This is my game uniform, my *only* uniform. Now you know why she didn't want me to wear it."

"I'm sorry."

"Sorry's not good enough." Sam stewed for a moment, then softened. She had an idea. "You'll have to wash it for me."

I shrugged. "Sure. I'll give it to my mom to wash. No problem."

"Not your mom," Sam protested. "*You*. Your mom will tell mine what happened. You need to wash my uniform—and not at home. Go to a laundromat."

"A laundromat? Forget it! I only came here to help you sell candy."

"Sell candy?" Sam rolled her eyes. "You came here to get coins. Don't lie."

"That reminds me," I said. I wanted to see my treasure one more time. I reached my hand into my empty pocket. Then it hit me. The pay phone. My 1932 quarter. "NO!"

I pushed a wrinkled dollar bill into the coin changer. The machine sent it right back to me. "Just take it!" I ordered. I straightened the dollar bill and tried again. This time four quarters clinked into the change tray at the bottom. I quickly checked the dates. No keepers.

"Can I borrow one of those?" Felix asked. He sat on a dryer staring at the readout on his pager. "I need to make a call."

I thought about it. "You'll pay me back?"

"Of course. I'm loaded."

I tossed Felix a quarter. He strutted to the pay phone like he owned the laundromat. It was nice to see him in such a good mood, unlike me. The pond incident was an accident. I still couldn't believe I had to wash Sam's uniform. With $3.00 worth of change in my pocket, I found an empty machine. The uniform went in first, followed by prewash, detergent, and even some bleach. By the time I got it going, Felix was off the phone and back in my face.

"That was Mitch. He placed an order. Do you have another quarter?"

"What for? You just talked to Mitch."

"I got another page while I was on the phone."

"I didn't hear it."

"I set my pager to vibrate," Felix explained, extending his palm. "Wait a second. You better make that two quarters. I just got paged again."

"I don't believe this." I grudgingly gave him two quarters.

Felix jogged to the phone and dialed the number. I wanted to gag just listening to him.

"Who loves you, Baby?" he spouted off. "No problem ... I gotcha covered ... That's right ... you're my man!" He sounded more like a Hollywood agent than my best friend. As soon as he hung up, he was back on the phone. He had barely finished with that call when another page came in. He motioned for me to toss him another quarter. I felt like throwing it at him as fast as Sam pitched, but I controlled myself and put it in the slot for him. With a few dollar bills left, at least I had another reason to get more quarters from the bill changer.

This time the machine gobbled down both bills on the first try. I carefully examined all eight quarters. One had potential, a 1951-P.

I tried to show Felix but he waved me off, too engrossed in his call. When he hung up, he still didn't have time to look at it. "Word travels fast when it comes to candy discounts. I'm the most popular kid in town."

"Until everyone's sick of candy or broke."

"You're just jealous," Felix said. He put out his hand. "Another quarter, Dude."

"Speaking of broke, this pay phone stuff has got to go. This is the last one you'll get from me." I put a quarter in his hand then intentionally turned my back. Good thing I did. Crusher walked in front of the laundromat.

"Felix! Crusher's out there!" I dropped behind a washing machine. "If he finds me in here doing a *girl's* laundry, I'll never live it down."

"Relax. Me and Crusher are like this," Felix said, crossing his fingers. "Besides, I'm not doing any laundry. I'll cover for you."

I peered over the machine, just as Crusher grabbed the glass door at the front of the laundromat. He must have seen Felix. I had to act fast.

10

The Static Clown

I waddled to an industrial dryer in the back of the laundromat and squeezed behind it. Unfortunately it was on, and I accidentally knocked loose the exhaust hose. Hot air rushed over my face and hair. It felt like I was standing behind a jet engine. I couldn't hear much of what Felix and Crusher were talking about, but they were both happy. I've never heard Crusher laugh so much.

"That's a good one, Felix," he said. "You crack me up."

I wasn't sure, but it sounded like Crusher said they should hang out more. Felix took it all in stride. I think he even asked Crusher for a quarter. "Anytime," I heard Crusher say.

I couldn't believe it. My face was melting and my hair was disintegrating, just so Crusher wouldn't see me washing Sam's clothes. But Felix was rapping with the guy like they were best friends. By the time

Crusher left, my legs hurt so much from squatting, I could barely stand up. I steadied myself with the row of washers as I limped toward Felix.

He looked in my direction and let out a laugh. "Nice hair, Willie."

"What are you talking about?" I hobbled to the mirror on the side wall. One look and I wanted to hide. A red funnel cloud had parked on my head. I tried to mat it down but once I lifted my hand, every hair returned to an upright position.

"You look like Bozo, the static clown," Felix joked.

"Static huh?" I moved to Felix and touched his arm. *Zap!*

"Ouch!" Felix complained. "What'd you do that for?"

"For not getting rid of Crusher sooner."

"I didn't turn you in, did I?" Felix looked at his pager then picked up the phone.

"Don't even think of asking me for a quarter," I told him.

"I don't need one. My *real* friend, Crusher, gave me plenty." Felix dialed and switched to his Hollywood agent voice.

Stewing, I returned to the washing machine to check on Sam's clothes. After a few minutes the cycle finished. They came out clean, so I tossed them into a dryer. Then I made my way to the front and scanned Main Street through the full-length windows of the laundromat. Plummet's Hobbies was across the street and down a few stores. Next to it was Classic Coins.

I checked my watch: 7:00 P.M. My dad and Mr. Speer had both locked up an hour ago. The stores were dark. Reaching down, I picked up a magazine to browse, but as soon as I opened the cover, I noticed someone in a white truck easing past Classic Coins. The driver's neck looked like rubber as he twisted around to watch the store. There was something familiar about him.

When he turned around, my heart stopped. It was Jack South. I squinted to confirm the details. He had a narrow face with bushy brown hair on the sides. This time I had no doubt. It was him, and he was casing Classic Coins.

I moved to the window, determined to get a closer look. South turned in my direction. I raised the magazine to cover my face. I would have needed a newspaper to cover my funnel-cloud hair, but hopefully that wouldn't matter.

Once South passed, I lowered the magazine to get the license plate number on his truck. I made out the first three letters before he turned left at the corner. "Felix," I shouted. "I'm going after the white truck. It's Jack South, the guy the police are after. Keep an eye on Sam's clothes. You can't let them overheat in the dryer."

Felix nodded and pretended to shoot me with his index finger and thumb.

"Does that mean yes?" I asked, pushing open the door.

Felix covered the phone. "You got it, Dano. Book 'em."

Before I grabbed the door, Felix was back on the phone. I doubted he knew what he had agreed to, but I had to trust him. South was getting away. I pushed my stiff legs as fast as they would go and rounded the corner. The white truck was stopped behind a minivan. Perfect. I hid behind a telephone pole while memorizing the license plate. Then I sprinted back to the laundromat. As I reached the corner, the truck whipped a U-turn and came toward me. I made it to the laundromat just in time. When the truck neared Classic Coins, he slowed down again to watch the store.

"Felix! I need the phone now!" I ordered.

He held up his hand, like I would have to wait. "You got it, big spender," he said into the receiver.

I grabbed the phone. "I've got to call the police."

"It's Plummet … He's spazzing again," Felix told the person on the other end. "Don't sweat it."

That was it. I yanked the phone from Felix. "Later, Babe," I barked into the receiver. I slammed it down then popped a quarter into the slot. Felix stared at me in shock. I dialed the police station as fast as I could. It seemed like Sutton would never come to the phone. When he heard my voice, he nearly hung up.

"Not again, Plummet," he moaned. It sounded like he slapped his forehead.

"I'm certain this time." I gave him the license number and the description of the driver. That got Sutton's attention.

"I'll run the plate. If it checks out, we'll send a car over."

"Should I keep watch?" I asked, ready to do my part.

"If you want. But if we don't show up soon, forget it."

As soon as I hung up, Felix grabbed the phone again. "Sounds like a real emergency. Thanks for hanging up on one of my biggest customers."

"It *was* an emergency! Sutton will find out soon enough." I returned to the window to watch for the truck. After a moment it returned, this time driving faster than before. At the corner, it turned right and disappeared out of sight. I watched the street in both directions. I pressed my face against the window to see as far as I could. But the truck never returned, and the police never arrived.

Then I smelled something burning.

"Oh no," I said, running for the dryer. I flung open the door and grabbed Sam's uniform. It felt like it was on fire. "Felix!" I tossed the uniform on the counter across from the dryer. One look at the fabric and I wanted to cry. The letters that spelled Sam's last name

were melted together. I carefully peeled them apart.
"NO!"

Felix finally hung up and came over. "What's wrong, Champ?"

"You were supposed to take this out of the dryer. Now look at it."

"It's not that messed up."

"Look at it!" The *e* in Stewart had oozed into the *t* except for a little dot. "It doesn't spell Stewart anymore, Felix. It spells St. wart."

Felix thought for a moment. "St. is an abbreviation for Saint. It looks like Sam's new name is Saint Wart."

"That's right. When Sam is on the mound they'll chant, 'Wart! Wart! Wart!' They'll call her the patron saint of skin fungus."

"That's not my fault. You should have checked it yourself when you got back. You put it in the dryer. There's only one of me to go around. Everyone wants a piece of me."

"Oh, I want a piece of you all right." It was all I could do not to grab Felix and throw *him* in the dryer.

"If you weren't so busy playing junior detective, you wouldn't have melted Sam's uniform."

"If you weren't so busy playing junior tycoon, you wouldn't have melted her uniform."

"I'm raising money for the team. At least I'm trying to help her."

"What do you think *I'm* doing?"

"You're just here to find coins. Admit it."

The word "coins" triggered something in my mind. I frantically checked my pockets. "NO! Not again!" I had used the rare quarter to call the police. Going to the phone, I thumped it with my fist. "Gimme my quarter back." *Bam! Bam! Bam!*

"Plummet! Stop that!" a deep voice boomed. I turned to see Officer Sutton standing in the doorway. "You may have been right this time. The truck plate you gave us was stolen."

I looked across the street then back at Sutton, who seemed ready to take me seriously—finally. It may have cost me a prize quarter, but at least this time it was worth it.

For the next few days I barely spoke to Felix. I was too mad about Sam's uniform. Sam wasn't all that happy either. When I brought it to her, I focused on how clean it was. Then I quickly mentioned the name problem. "The *e* got a little messed up, that's all."

Sam stared at the letters. I hoped she wouldn't put two and two together. She did.

"St. wart? That's Saint Wart! They'll kill me on the mound. I'll be the laughingstock of the league."

"All jokes wear off," I reasoned. "By next season no one will remember."

That didn't help much, so Sam gave me the same silent treatment I was giving Felix. With no friends to hang out with, I had plenty of time to look for coins. If only I could find one worth keeping. No matter how many piggy banks and change drawers I picked through, I struck out. All I came up with was pennies worth a penny and nickels worth a nickel.

The more I thought about it, the more I knew I needed to forgive Felix. I had messed up so many times through the years, and Jesus always forgave me. I owed Felix the same treatment. I also knew I needed to ask Sam to forgive me. Those verses Felix read really stuck in my head. I hadn't been that kind of friend at all.

The tough thing would be getting through to Felix. His candy business had made him the most popular guy in school. Kids crowed around him wherever he went—in the hall, in class, in the cafeteria. I decided my best bet was to put a note in his locker. Tearing a piece of white lined paper from my notebook, I wrote down my request. I asked him to meet me in the auditorium in the same place he tried to scare the hiccups out of me.

Just before second period, I dropped the note through the vent in his locker. To make sure he read it, I decided to return after class to watch for his response. The moment the bell rang, I practically sprinted through the halls to take up my position. I stood on the stairs a short way from his locker. As students converged on their lockers, Felix rounded the corner with his crowd of groupies. He was the center of attention and eating it up.

"I gotcha covered, Crusher. You're the man," Felix spouted off.

Crusher wouldn't hear of it. "No, Felix, *you're* the man."

"No, Crush, *you're* the man," Felix fired back.

"No, *you're* the man. The Lix-Man."

"No, you're the—" Felix stopped and grinned. "The Lix-Man, huh? I like that." At that point they both busted up. Crusher patted Felix on the back then left his arm on his shoulder. I wanted to gag.

"The Lix-Man rules," a seventh grader said.

"Felix for president," another added.

"King Felix," a kid threw out.

Only a few students had problems with him, and even they were nice about it. "Felix, no offense, but you didn't call me back."

"Yeah," a cute blonde added. "Did you get my page?"

"Sorry, about that. But I've got a solution." Felix dialed the combination on his locker then opened the door and reached inside. But what he produced wasn't my note.

Beam Me Up, Felix

Faces glowed with admiration. Felix flipped open a high-tech handset. For a moment I thought he'd say, "Beam me up, Scotty." The green numbers on the key pad glowed.

"A cell phone?" Crusher was impressed.

"You got it, Bro," Felix said. "No more missed pages. You want the Lix-Man, just dial my number. I'll be ready—24/7—to take your order."

"Cool."

"Awesome."

"Psycho."

Felix handed out chocolate-colored business cards with his number on them. Then the cell phone rang. "Yeah, Lix-Man here. What? No problem. Got ya' covered, Babe."

"Who was that?" a kid asked.

"Megan Yenny, high school cheerleader. She's a babe, and she placed an order."

"Oowee," Crusher marvelled. "A high school cheerleader."

"I've got friends in high places," Felix offered with a grin. Opening his locker, he handed out candy. He filled orders and even tossed out a few treats "on the house." I waited for him to find my note, but he never did. It probably fell on the ground and got trampled under the feet of his admiring public.

Looking down from the stairs, I wondered if Felix even remembered my name. It didn't seem like it. I leaned on the rail and dropped my head, feeling mad and lonely.

"What's with you?" a voice asked. Sam sidled up next to me.

"The name's Willie."

"I know your name."

"Just checking. Are you here to chew me out again for what happened to your uniform?"

"No, I'm here to say I forgive you. You said you were sorry, and I should have forgiven you then. But I was so mad."

"I understand. What'd your mom say?"

"She was ticked, and I got grounded for two days. But she's fine now. She even came up with a solution—one of those iron-on letters. The replacement e looks almost the same." Sam and I talked things over for a few minutes. I said I was sorry again. Then I told her about my failed plan to meet with Felix.

"Why don't you just go up and talk to him?" Sam asked. "Felix is in a great mood. He even gave me some candy." Sam held out a handful of M&M's. "Just wave him over."

At first I refused. Then I gave it a try. I waved at Felix when he looked in my direction. But it didn't help. He couldn't see past all the candy-crazed kids mingling around him. "We've got to get his attention. You have the great arm, Sam. Bounce an M&M off his head."

Sam shrugged and took aim. The first toss hit the top of a locker. The second just missed Felix's head and landed in an open backpack.

"Come on pitcher, zing one in there," I urged.

Sam wound up. The M&M flew at Mitch's head. He looked around confused.

"Sam, what's your problem?" I complained.

"If you think it's so easy, you try it." She handed me the M&M's.

I wound up and let one fly. It connected with Crusher's temple. He turned toward me, his eyes cold as ice. I couldn't help weaseling out of it. I tipped my head toward Sam. Crusher shifted his attention to her, but the ice in his eyes melted. He blushed and offered a half smile, like he just wanted her to see the teeth *not* covered with candy.

At first Sam wasn't sure what was happening. She just stared at Crusher. Then she wanted to kill me.

"You told him I threw it?" she snapped, her face red.

"I didn't say a thing."

"But you implied it," Sam went on. She slugged me in the arm while chewing me out. She didn't calm down until Crusher returned his attention to Felix. I rubbed my sore arm, thinking maybe I would have been better off facing Crusher. "OK, so maybe M&M tossing wasn't the best approach. There's got to be something I can do."

"Too bad you don't have the hiccups," Sam told me, popping an M&M in her mouth. "Felix wouldn't leave you alone back then."

"That's it. I'll get near Felix and fake the hiccups. That'll get his attention." I slid down the stair rail and weaved my way through the students. When I was just a few feet from Felix, I let one fly. "*Hiccup.*"

The kids next to me turned for a second, but no one else seemed to notice. I squeezed between two seventh-grade girls and tried again. This time I really let it go. "*HIC.*" I knew Felix heard me, but he pretended I wasn't alive. Seconds later I went again. "*HICCUP.*"

Thanks to Mrs. McNelly's acting class, I was in top form. "*HIC ... HICCUP.*"

Felix couldn't ignore me forever. Kids winced like I was grossing them out, but I didn't care. I stepped closer. "*HICCUP.*"

That was as far as I got.

"Put a sock in it!" Felix said. He spouted off like he was talking to a stray dog.

"Yeah, put Plummet out of his misery," Crusher chimed in. A few of his friends stepped between me and Felix. That was enough for me. I returned to Sam, licking my wounds.

"Well, what'd he say?" Sam asked.

"Put a sock in it," I snapped.

"What?" Sam asked, looking hurt. As if things weren't bad enough, Sam thought I was saying that to her.

When I entered Classic Coins that afternoon, a customer passed me on the way out. Mr. Speer stood behind the glass counter. He held a quarter in one hand. With the other he held a magnifying viewer to his eye. "Unbelievable."

"What is it?" I asked.

"A 1916 Standing Liberty quarter. The extremely fine grade makes it worth $2,800."

"For a quarter? Why can't I find something like that?" I put down my backpack and stared at the coins under the glass. I had come directly from school, as frustrated as ever. "All the quarters I find are worth a quarter. Except for the two I lost."

"You're having trouble holding onto coins. First the 50¢: piece, now quarters."

"I'm having even more trouble holding onto friends." I explained the problems I was having with Felix and Sam.

"If the contest has anything to do with it, drop out. A good friend is worth more than a good coin, any day."

I knew Mr. Speer was right. From the night of the anniversary celebration until now, my coin search had come between me and my friends. It wasn't intentional or that obvious, but it was true. Still staring at the coins under the glass, I closed my eyes to get a different perspective. I pictured Felix and Sam and everything we had been through together. I asked God to forgive me and show me how to make it up to them.

"I'll say this," Mr. Speer went on, "all friendships have their ups and downs, but if you're willing to try, you'll find a way to work things out."

"I'm definitely willing," I said. "But even when I try, it doesn't help. Why can't they come to me for once?"

"I'm sure they could, but you might wait a while. You're always better off taking the first step toward restoring a friendship than waiting for someone else to do it."

"Maybe you're right," I said. "It would be nice to stop losing friends *and* coins."

"You've mentioned lost coins twice now. What are you talking about?"

At first I hesitated, not sure I wanted to alarm Mr. Speer. But I decided better safe than sorry. I explained what happened at the mansion and the laundromat.

Mr. Speer rolled the magnifying glass between his fingers. "You saw Jack South drive by my store? Have the police found the truck?"

I shook my head. "Officer Sutton said they haven't turned up a thing."

Mr. Speer searched through the front window then tightened his lips. "Well, I'm sure crooks have thought of robbing this place before, but no one ever has. The locks are good. The place is secure. I'm not going to worry about it."

"Are you sure this place is safe?"

"You've seen the steel grid I pull in front of the windows each night. Even if someone breaks the glass, there's no way to get in. Twenty years in business and not one break-in. Classic Coins will be okay. But thanks for keeping an eye out for me."

"Sure," I said. "Now if I can just keep an eye out for coins worth more than their face value."

"You've still got three days. Don't give up. You must have found a few winners by now."

I explained what I had and that I still needed a quarter and 50¢ piece. "So what do you think? Am I still in the running?"

"I'm not going to lie to you. It won't be easy. I've seen some pretty impressive finds by the other kids."

"Like Crusher's 50¢ piece that should have been mine."

"That, and a blonde kid had a mint condition Susan B. Anthony dollar. He found it in the cash register at his dad's hardware store."

He was talking about Mitch. I knew it. His dad managed the giant warehouse hardware store out on the highway. Mitch could look through millions of coins per day. Compared to the one tray in Plummet's Hobbies, I didn't stand a chance. "I might as well give up."

"Don't give up, Willie," Mr. Speer went on. "You'll do fine. Besides, it's only for lunch."

"It's not about the lunch. I want to win. It's like when I play Monopoly with my friends. It's just nice to come out on top. I know Sam feels that way about her softball games."

"I can appreciate that. But it's like I said, don't give up."

Mr. Speer was right. And I knew it. Even though it was only one little change tray, I decided to head next door to Plummet's Hobbies and check the register. When I got there, Dad was in the model aircraft aisle, helping a customer. Once I made sure he saw that it was me, I opened the register and started with the quarters.

The guy talking to my dad had his back to me. At first I ignored their conversation. Then, the guy said something that surprised me. He asked if we stayed around after closing. At least I think that's what he said. I couldn't make out the rest. But it must have been convincing because my dad didn't bat an eye.

"Once we lock up, we're gone," Dad explained.

I stared at the guy's hair. Something didn't seem right. I leaned forward, wanting to see as many details as possible. The brown neck hairs didn't match the ones on top.

"Well, I'll have to hurry back," he said, his back still to me. "This will do it for now."

He handed my dad a model of a military transport plane. Dad headed for the register. Once he turned, I tried not to stare. I looked away, but checked back. He wore thick glasses with black frames. His reddish-brown hair lacked a part. "Something wrong?" he asked.

Dad cleared his throat and answered for me. "My son's eyes are a little out of focus after looking at so many coins." He explained the contest at Classic Coins. The guy listened politely, watching me and my dad at the same time. He had a wide nose, cleft in his chin, and a blotchy tan.

That was enough for me. He was Jack South, disguised. He had to be. I stepped aside with my handful of quarters, picking through each one. The dates meant nothing to me. All I could think about was peeking at his face. His mustache looked too red for the dark brown stubble on his chin.

The guy thanked my dad, then gave me one last smile before leaving. As soon as he got outside, my dad turned on me. "What was that all about? You made him feel really uncomfortable."

"I couldn't help it. Something about him didn't look right. The hair on top of his head didn't match the hair on his neck. He was—"

"Willie, it's called a toupee," my dad shot back. "Some bald men wear them. You know better than to stare."

"It was more than that. His mustache looked wrong. And he had a cleft in his chin. He was Jack South!" I ran out front and looked up and down the street. South was gone. Unwilling to give up, I checked the alley and a few side streets. Nothing.

My dad was waiting for me when I returned to the store. "I think someone has stared at too many coins."

I told him all about South and the stolen truck. My dad decided that if Mr. Speer wasn't too concerned, we shouldn't be. It made sense. Why would South want to steal a bunch of models? We didn't have enough money in our register to make it worth his while, especially compared to Classic Coins next door. Still, I couldn't shake the feeling that Jack South had just paid us a visit and that it wasn't the first time.

Eventually, I returned my attention to the quarters in my hand. I searched through each one, checking the date and the location of the mint. If they weren't of value, I put them in the register. I was almost done when one seemed to have potential. It was a 1937-S. I looked it up in the book and nearly fainted. It was worth at least $10.00. I jumped up and down. My dad celebrated with me. I couldn't wait to go next door and show Mr. Speer. He was right. Even when things look bad, *don't give up*.

A Sticky Situation

When Sam stepped onto the pitcher's mound, my stomach got queasy. It was the second to last game of the season. If they won today, they'd only need one more win to make the play-offs. They were facing the Blue Jays, their rivals from Ashland, a town about 30 miles a way. But none of that made me queasy. All I could think about was the *e* Sam's mom had ironed on the back of her jersey. So far it looked fine, but the game had just started. The other team watched Sam like vultures, looking for any weakness to pounce on. The last thing she needed was to hear *St. Wart*.

Sam held her feet together and the softball in front of her. She stared at the catcher waiting for a sign. The batter bent her knees, ready for the pitch. Stepping forward, Sam whipped her arm under and let it fly.

"Stee-rike!" the umpire hollered. The batter didn't budge.

Teammates and parents cheered for Sam. So did I. That was a good start. The next pitch didn't do as well, but by the fifth pitch the umpire yelled, "Steerike three." Sam never looked back. She pitched like a pro, with speed and accuracy, retiring the side. By the fourth inning, Sam's team was ahead 2–0.

With things going so well, I decided to head to the Snack Shack for a cold drink. As soon as Sam finished batting, I made my way over. On the way, all I could think about was what to say to Felix. He was working today. This could be our first chance to talk in days. He was still Mr. Popular. Kids crowded around him at school and he filled orders or took new ones. When I called he was either out or on his cell phone.

The pace must have been hard on him. His eyes looked weary and dim. He smiled less. I wanted to help him, but he acted too important to let me try. How sad, I thought. Felix found the popularity he was looking for but lost his friends and happiness on the way.

As I stepped along, watching the grass for coins, I heard a commotion coming from the direction of the Snack Shack. I couldn't see what was going on until I rounded a little league field. Then I kicked into a full sprint. An angry mob surrounded the Snack Shack. It looked like they wanted to lynch the guy inside, namely Felix. A woman with grey hair shouted over the counter, as if ready to climb in and get him.

I barreled ahead, not sure what to do. Part of me wanted to say, "Serves you right, Mr. Cool, Mr. Lix-

Man." But I knew that was no way to treat a friend. I wanted to help, maybe *now* he would let me. First I had to find out what the ruckus was about. As I got closer, I realized the crowd was split in two. One group clamored at the back door. I recognized most of them from school. Crusher and his thugs were closest to the Snack Shack, making threats. A girl in a green cheerleading uniform stood behind them, but she wasn't cheering. Others kicked the red dirt, grumbling.

In front of the Snack Shack, parents and grandparents took up the siege. They crowded around the window, pointing at something inside. Maybe it wasn't the right thing to do, maybe Felix didn't want my help, but I couldn't stand back and do nothing. Moving fast, I snaked my way through the kids. "Coming through! Coming through!" I said with confidence. Before Crusher and the others knew what had happened, I slipped into the Snack Shack.

Felix stood guard over a several boxes of candy. He extended his arms like wings. With one hand he held off the adults, with the other, the kids.

"What's going on?" I asked, not knowing if Felix would be glad to see me or not. Maybe he'd even tell *me* to get out.

"The manager made a mistake," he said in desperation. "When she saw these boxes, she didn't order more."

I found myself holding up both hands like Felix, trying to fend off the mobs. "So? It's candy, isn't it? Just sell it!"

"It's not that easy. I ordered these boxes for the kids at school. And they're here to collect—at a discount."

"I thought you could only sell at a discount *away* from the ballpark."

Felix shut his eyes tight, as if that was the last thing he wanted to hear. "I blew it, all right? Things got so hectic, I told them they could pick up their orders here. But when the teams heard that this candy wasn't for sale, and that it was reserved for kids buying at a discount, they went berserk. They went straight for the adults."

I glanced at the parents beating their fists on the counter and understood. It was like a PTA meeting gone bad. Talk about a sticky situation! Only one order of candy, and two mobs that wanted it—at a discount. I thought of Felix's cell phone. "Have you called the manager?"

"She wouldn't answer," Felix blurted out, keeping his voice down. "The soonest I can have more product delivered is Monday. I'm toast. If I sell the candy to the parents, Crusher and his friends will string me up. If I sell the candy at a discount to Crusher, the parents will get me. Either way I'm a goner."

That was all I needed to hear. Felix needed my help and whether he asked for it or not, I would stand in the gap for him. Swallowing hard, I stepped to the back door and faced Crusher's crowd. "You can pick up your orders from Felix after school on Monday. If you can't wait, go around to the window and pay the price listed on the menu board."

"Yeah, right!" Crusher growled. It felt like I was standing beneath a grizzly bear, just robbed of a cub.

"Tell him, Felix," I said, my heart pounding.

Felix moved toward me, his arms still extended. "That's right, Crusher. I messed up."

"That's your problem. I want my candy," Crusher whined.

"You heard him, Crusher!" I barked, sounding like Officer Sutton. So much for Willie the chicken. No one was "bawking" now. I gritted my teeth, not knowing if Crusher would pop me in the mouth or back off. Either way, I wouldn't back down. Felix was my friend, and he needed my help. "Back up! Back up!"

Crusher stepped back in shock. I quickly shut the door and locked it before Crusher realized who had bossed him around. Then I turned to Felix and whispered. "Tell the adults we're open for business at the prices marked."

The parents greeted Felix's announcement with hesitation. I think the idea of a discount had gotten to them too. A few wandered off, but others started buying. I stepped to the counter and took orders. Felix ripped open boxes and handed me the candy. We worked well together and the line moved fast. An elderly woman even gave me a 50¢ piece as a tip. Once things got under control, Felix told me I could leave. I offered to stay longer, but he turned me down.

As I headed to the rear of the Snack Shack, I thought about Crusher and his friends. They were probably waiting to lynch me instead of Felix. Pausing at the back door, I slowly unlocked it and stepped outside. They were gone. The thought of paying full price had scared them off.

I waited before closing the door, to watch Felix. I thought maybe he'd thank me or say goodbye. He didn't. Even after I had walked away from the Snack Shack, I kept looking back, hoping he'd give me a wave from the window. That didn't happen either. It bummed me out, but I didn't regret helping him. Felix was my friend and always would be. If Jesus could lay down His life for His friends, I could stand up for one of mine.

Sam watched me nibble at a piece of pizza. Her team won the game and she asked me to come along for the celebration. I did my best to compliment Sam on how well she pitched. But she could tell I wasn't happy and that it would take more than a thick slice of pepperoni and a cold root beer to cheer me up.

"Felix will be his old self by tomorrow. You wait," Sam told me.

I shook my head. "Monday afternoon he'll fill everyone's orders and be the Lix-Man again."

"But for how long?" Sam argued. "Kids can't buy bulk candy forever. Eventually their teeth will rot."

"Not if they brush right and floss," I said, in no mood to agree.

Sam stared at the ceiling. "I give up." With that she moved to another table to mingle with her team-mates.

I sat alone, feeling miserable. Eventually, I got out the 50¢ piece that I had received as a tip. I had already checked the date, but thought I'd look it over again. It was a 1976-D. I doubted it was worth more than 50¢, but at least it completed my collection. I checked the details on Eisenhower's face. The ears were fine, the cheeks raised. It had potential. But I wouldn't know until I checked my coin reference book. I had left it at Plummet's Hobbies next to the register.

I opened wide and downed the rest of my pizza and root beer. Before leaving, I congratulated the A's and their coach.

"It all comes down to Tuesday's game. You'll be there, right?" Sam asked.

"Of course I'll be there. I'm your—*hiccup*—friend, aren't I?" I slapped my forehead in frustration. "Not again."

"Next time try chewing the pizza before you swallow it," Sam smirked. "Where are you going in such a rush?"

I told her where and why. "If I'm still there—*hic-cup*—when you leave, stop by." With that I headed for Plummet's Hobbies. It was only a block away. Saturday night meant dark store fronts. The alley in back of the store was even darker. Arriving at the door, I lifted the letter *c* from the mat to get the secret key.

It was gone. My fingers slid over the rough mat. Where could it be? It didn't make sense. I stepped back and looked around. There wasn't a person in sight, just a few parked cars, an empty dumpster, and a white truck. A white truck? My heart kicked into overdrive. I recognized the truck from the other day. It was the one Jack South was driving.

Part of me wanted to run for my life. But I moved back to the door. I had to check. I grabbed the knob and turned. It was locked. I was about to take off when I noticed something. The door wasn't closed all the way. A pack of matches wedged under the door kept it from latching.

Adrenaline pumped through me. I stared at the door, not sure what to do. Then I thought of Sutton. Of course, I had to call him. I turned to go. But I didn't get far. A moan coming from inside stopped me. Muffled words followed. Someone was in trouble! The voice sounded familiar. I stared at the door again. My heart thumped like a jackhammer. If I went for help now, it might be too late for the person inside.

I grabbed the knob and slowly opened the door.

The Coin Caper

A dim light over the lab workbench lit the room just enough for me to see. Felix struggled against ropes wrapped around his chest, hands, and feet. A red bandanna covered his mouth. His glasses were beside him, shattered.

I rushed to him and started on the bandanna. The knot felt like a rock, but I eventually got it loose. "Where's South?" I asked. My fingers trembled as I yanked to untie his feet.

"He's in Classic Coins," Felix gasped. "He went through your wall."

"The wall?" I muttered in shock. But as I strained at the knots, I realized that it all made sense. The customer who said "knock on wood" and the one who asked my dad about closing time were both South, just as I suspected. He had disguised himself at least two times, maybe more.

"Why are—*hiccup*—you here?" I asked Felix.

"Sshhh!" Felix warned. "I came looking for you. When I got here the back door was wedged open, so I came inside. That's when South jumped me. I wanted to thank you for helping me, and tell you I was sorry for the way I've been acting.".

"No problem, Dude," I said. It felt good to hear Felix apologize.

"I remembered the Bible verses I read you," Felix went on. "I decided that if being popular means losing my *real* friends, it's not worth it."

I nodded with conviction. Now if we could just get away before South got to us. I struggled with the knot on Felix's ankles, but it wouldn't budge. I'd have to cut the rope. Before getting a knife, I thought of something. "Do you still have your cell phone?"

"Sure. In my coat pocket." Felix nodded to the right side.

I dialed 911 and wedged the phone between Felix's shoulder and chin. "Tell them to—*hiccup*—send help. I'm going for a knife." With my mouth shut tight, I searched the lab. I looked everywhere but it was no use; I couldn't find anything. With time running out, I knew what I had to do. I crept like a spider to the front of the store. I found the hole right where South had knocked when he came disguised as a customer. Sawdust and powdered drywall covered the carpet beneath it. The hole was just big enough for a man to squeeze through. As I passed it, I could hear the sound of coins jingling next door.

Crawling to the counter, I quickly removed an Exacto knife, used for cutting balsa wood. It was razor sharp. But just as I started back, South dropped a sack of coins on our side. I stood still, thinking he would come through too, but he didn't. He remained in Classic Coins, gathering more treasure.

I exhaled in relief. Too bad that involved opening my mouth. "HICCUP!" I slapped my hand over my mouth, but it was too late.

"What's going on in there?" South grumbled.

I stepped around the bag of coins and ran to the back room. The cell phone was on the floor next to Felix. "Sutton's on his way."

"So is South," I told him. We heard another bag drop, followed by grunting and scraping. He was squirming through the hole to get us.

I cut the rope around Felix's ankles and pulled him to his feet. Ropes still held his hands behind his back, but they would have to wait. We pushed open the back door and crashed right into Sam. All three of us fell to the ground.

"What's going on?" she asked from the pavement.

"No time to—*hiccup*—explain!" I scrambled to my feet and pulled Felix up with me. "Move it." We sprinted through the alley in the opposite direction of South's truck. "In here," I ordered, pulling Felix between two buildings. Sam followed.

We waited. Nothing. Only silence trailed behind us. I chanced a peek back. South barged from the back door of Plummet's Hobbies and hurried to the white truck. He carried two bags of coins. That's why it took him so long. He didn't care about us. He wanted to get away with the silver and gold.

"Well?" Sam asked.

"He's taking off!" I told them. Sam and Felix looked around the corner. I remembered what happened the last time South sped off in the white truck. He got away. "We've got to stop him!"

"Us?" Felix sputtered. "What about the police? They're on the way!"

"What if they don't get here in time? Do you hear—HICCUP—any sirens?" I asked.

"All I hear is your hiccups," Sam said.

"See!" I pleaded. "It's up to us."

South tossed the coin bags in the cab of the truck then jumped in after them. He screeched to the end of the alley and turned left.

"Where do you think he's going?" Sam asked.

"My guess is out of town, by side streets," I reasoned. "Come on! We can cut him off." I darted across the alley. I wove my way through buildings and parked cars. Sam and Felix followed. I kept sprinting all the way to Baker Street. "He's got to come by here."

"You're probably right," Sam gasped, trying to catch her breath. "But how will *we* stop him?"

"I don't know," I said, getting frustrated. I searched the ground between the buildings and came up with a few rocks and a chunk of brick. "Maybe these won't stop him, but a broken windshield will definitely slow him down."

Sam grabbed a big rock from me. "Ready when you are."

With Felix's hands still tied, he couldn't throw. We sent him to the corner, to let us know when South appeared.

"He's coming," Felix called out.

"Ready?" I asked Sam.

She nodded. The white truck peeled around the corner. I stepped out from the brick building and let a rock fly. It smacked the front grill but missed the glass. The truck bore down. Sam chucked her rock, but it missed entirely. I quickly threw another. Way off.

"He's almost here!" I said.

"Watch out, Willie." Sam said. She stood with her feet together and a chunk of brick in her hand. I knew what was coming. It was game time, and Sam was on the mound. She held the brick in front of her like a softball. The truck bore down. Thirty feet away. Twenty. Sam whipped her arm under and stepped forward. If the truck was going 60, the brick left her hand at 70. Sam might as well have fired a canon. The brick shot straight for the windshield, shattering the glass on impact. South swerved out of control and crashed into a lamp post.

Within seconds, Sutton pulled up along with another squad car. South stumbled from the truck in a daze, his loose legs wobbling beneath him. When Officer Sutton snapped on the handcuffs, South didn't resist.

"We'll see how he likes it," Felix said, returning to us. He quickly added, "Nice throw, Sam."

"That's for sure," I said. "Way to go."

Once South was in the police car, we approached the crashed truck and filled Sutton in on what happened. "I'm impressed," he said, shaking his head in amazement. "Definitely impressed." As he filled out the report, other officers came over and congratulated us.

"Good thing Willie came along, or I would have been a goner," Felix told everyone.

I shrugged, "You would have done the same thing for me."

Felix shook his head and looked away from me, like he had spotted someone in the distance. "Not the Lix-Man. But he's gone. The real Felix is back. Now if you don't mind ..." Felix turned to expose his hands, still tied up.

"You got it, Dude." I had left the Exacto knife behind, so I worked at the ropes with my fingers. Sam helped and before long our best friend was free.

I stood at the glass counter in Classic Coins holding my breath. I didn't want to hiccup. Mr. Speer
looked over the sets of coins in front of him. All of us
waited with anticipation. Crusher looked like he
would put his fist through the glass or my face if he
didn't win. Felix had filled one last candy order, but
that was it. Crusher was having trouble getting by
without his daily dose of sugar.

Mr. Speer examined the coins from each of our
sets. A few coin collectors from town had come in to
see the results. They also wanted to show support for
Mr. Speer. The break-in really got to him. After 20
years of safety, he couldn't believe he nearly lost
everything. It made him reconsider his priorities.
Even though all of his coins were recovered, he realized he couldn't hold onto them forever. He hadn't
been to church in years, but knew enough about the
Bible to know that his values had gotten way out of
whack. "It's time I do something about it," he said,
vowing to store up treasures in heaven for a change.

I also took another look at what mattered. Of
course the Lord came first in my life. But friends were
near the top of my list too—definitely higher than a
coin, no matter what it was worth. I really wanted
Sam and Felix to come to the judging, but they didn't
make it. The break-in forced Mr. Speer to postpone
the judging a few days. It turned out to be the same
day as Sam's game. Felix wasn't clear on why he
couldn't make it, but I figured he had to work in the

Snack Shack. My plan was to head to the ball park as soon as the judging ended.

From what I could tell, Crusher would out-do me once again. He had a 1942-S quarter that looked like it left the mint yesterday. Other kids had impressive coins too. I glanced down at my set. It didn't look so hot, especially next to Crusher's. With the quarter he won at the Classic Coins celebration, and the 50¢ piece he found at the ball park, he would be tough to beat as always.

Mr. Speer put down the last coin and addressed us. "Well, gentlemen, I believe we have a winner."

Batter Up

Our eyes traveled back and forth between the sets and each other. "The first place set has a total value of $349.00."

I gasped along with everyone else. Then my heart fell. I knew the value of my coins. They weren't worth that. Crusher must have won again.

"Well, who is it?" Crusher gloated, already cocky.

Mr. Speer looked at each of us then smiled. "The winner is … Mr. Willie Plummet."

My mouth dropped. "HICCUP!"

"That's a strange way to celebrate," Mr. Speer said.

Everyone laughed and congratulated me. Except Crusher. "Plummet won? How? His coins didn't look that good."

Mr. Speer extended his magnifying glass to Crusher. "Take a closer look at the ear on Willie's dime. It's a double die. That makes it worth $300."

"Yes!" I let out. I jumped up and down, celebrating the win. I pounded on the wall and shouted, "I won, Dad. I won." He pounded back just as loud.

"I guess this means lunch is on me," Mr. Speer said. "And if you don't mind, I'd like to include your friends Felix and Sam. After what they did, that's the least I can do."

"Sounds good to me," I said, remembering where I wanted to go. I asked Mr. Speer to keep an eye on my coins, then took off for the ball park.

Felix wasn't in the Snack Shack, so I went straight for Sam's field. Good thing I did. Her game was practically over. Sam stood on the mound, eyeing the catcher. The runners on second and third led off.

Sam wound up and threw a strike.

"Way to—*hiccup*—go!" I shouted.

"Full count," the umpire said.

Sam checked the runners then threw another pitch. The batter swung and ripped the ball into left field. She only made it to first, but the runners on second and third scored. While the next batter headed for the plate, I hurried to the bleachers and sat down next to Sam's parents. "What's the score?"

"We're behind 8 to 11. They've got two outs," Mrs. Stewart told me. Then she quietly added, "We have one more at bat, then it's over."

I waited for a hiccup to pass before cheering. "Come on, Sam. You can do it."

Sam fired fastball after fastball. The batter seemed determined to swing at anything. She fouled away four pitches in a row. Sam eyed the catcher for the sign, then stepped into the wind-up. The pitch curved from the outside then headed for the plate.

The batter stepped into it, ready to smack it over the fence. She swung hard. *Whiff!*

"Stee—rike three. You're out," the umpire announced.

We burst into applause. I whistled. Parents chanted their kids' names to encourage them. Even though Sam's team was down by three runs, we knew they could come from behind and win.

Then the first batter struck out.

"That's OK," Mr. Stewart said. "We'll get 'em."

The second batter managed to get a walk, then steal second. But the third popped out. When the fourth batter stepped to the plate, a bleak silence held Sam's team. The other team was louder than ever. "One more to go," the girl playing second shouted. "Watch her whiff."

The girl at the plate kept looking back at the dugout, like she wished she was there. Her eyes were soft and nervous.

The pitcher sent a strike past her, then another. She looked too scared to swing at the ball even if it was resting on a tee.

"You can do it," the coach shouted out. "If it looks good, go for it."

The chatter got louder. "Hey batter. Hey batter!"

The pitcher wound up and let one fly. The girl brought the bat around. It looked like she was swinging in slow motion. But somehow she connected, barely. The ball dribbled down the third base line. The catcher scrambled after it while the runner headed for first. The catcher bobbled the ball then made a perfect throw.

We listened for the call.

"Safe!" the umpire shouted, spreading his hands. We exploded with cheers. The runner on second made it to third. When the next batter walked, we stared at the dugout. Sam was up, with bases loaded. She took a few practice swings while approaching the plate.

"Come on, Sam!" I shouted. "Show 'em what you've got."

Sam took another practice swing before entering the batter's box. That was a mistake. The *e* on her jersey dropped to the ground. I held my breath, hoping no one noticed but me. Wrong again.

"Nice name," a girl from the other team's dugout shouted. The girls on the field caught on and took up the taunt. "Whiff the wart!"

Sam glanced at her coach. He clapped and encouraged her. But that didn't help enough. She let a perfect pitch go by, one she could have smacked out of the park.

"Strike one," the umpire said.

The taunting increased. "Whiff the wart."

Fortunately, the next three pitches were balls. With the count 3–1, Sam got the green light to swing if it looked good. It didn't, but she went after it anyway.

"Stee-rike!" the umpire called out. "Full count."

That sent the other team into orbit. "Whiff the wart!"

Sam stepped away from the plate, and her coach motioned at her uniform. Sam didn't even bother to look. She just stared at the bleachers. Our eyes met for moment then she returned to the plate. I wanted to hide. Sam's biggest game of the season, and she had gone from star player to wart.

The pitcher stood with her feet together, the softball hidden in her glove.

"Whiff the Wart! Whiff the Wart!" the outfield chanted. Some of the people in the bleachers joined in. "Wart! Wart! Wart!"

I couldn't believe it. Talk about bad sportsmanship. Mr. and Mrs. Stewart were as shocked as I was. "You can do it, Samantha!" Mrs. Stewart called out.

But thanks to the "Wart" chant, *I* could barely hear her. There was no way Sam could. The pitcher stepped into the wind-up and let it fly. Sam swung but fouled it away.

"Whiff the Wart! Whiff the Wart! Whiff the Wart!"

I stared at my friend, feeling terrible. I had to help her. Standing up, I put my hands to my mouth. "Grand Slam Stewart! Grand Slam Stewart!" I wailed. Compared to the other team it didn't seem like much. But

I'd lose my voice shouting if I had to. Sam was my friend, and I would stick with her to the end.

I climbed to the top of the bleachers. I screamed as loud as I could. "Grand Slam Stewart! Grand Slam Stewart!" My throat burned. It felt as red as my hair. But I kept at it.

As the pitcher took the mound, Sam glanced back at me then bore down.

I carried on, waving my hands. I looked like an idiot and didn't care. This was for Sam. "Grand Slam Stewart!"

Pretty soon others joined in. We neared the volume of the other team.

"GRAND SLAM STEWART! GRAND SLAM STEWART!"

"WHIFF THE WART! WHIFF THE WART!"

Suddenly Felix appeared and climbed the bleachers beside me. He screamed even louder than I did. "GRAND SLAM STEWART!"

The pitcher whipped her arm around and under. The ball shot straight for the plate. Sam stepped into it and swung hard.

CRACK! The softball launched toward center. It kept going, and going, over the outfielder's head. We jumped up and down, screaming.

Sam rounded first and headed for second. The girls on second and third scored. Sam tagged second. The girl who was on first scored. The center fielder got to the ball and threw it to the cut-off. Sam rounded third and sprinted for home. The throw from the cut-off headed for the catcher. Sam lifted her arms and dove for the plate. The catcher caught the ball and brought it down.

We held our breath, waiting for the call.

"Safe!" the umpire yelled.

"YES!" I cheered.

"STEWART! STEWART! STEWART!" Felix screamed. We jumped up and down. I traded high fives with Mr. and Mrs. Stewart. Sam's team mobbed her at home. They piled on each other, laughing and rolling in the dirt. Finally, they got up and shook hands with the other team. Then the celebration moved to the bleachers. Sam hugged her parents, then put her arms around me and Felix.

"I'm sorry about your uniform," I said.

"It's okay," Sam told me. She put her ball cap on my head. "Thanks to Felix's fundraising efforts, we get new uniforms for the playoffs. Besides, Willie, you stood up for me when I needed it most."

"You could hear me?" I asked.

"Definitely. And Felix too at the end."

"Where were you before that?" I asked Felix. "I thought you'd be in the Snack Shack."

"I was. But when my shift ended, I went to get you a hiccup cure." He pulled a plastic cup from his backpack. "I got it from my neighbor, Mrs. Hamper."

Suddenly, I no longer felt like celebrating. "Thanks anyway, Felix, but my throat's kind of sore from shouting."

"It won't be after you drink this."

I looked Felix in the eye. "That's because I won't have a throat. The stuff *you* made practically melted it. This stuff will kill me."

"Come on, I'm your friend. Trust me." Felix removed the lid then placed a paper towel over the top. "The force needed to draw the recipe through the paper towel is what cures you."

"Go ahead, Willie," Sam added, putting her arm on Felix's shoulder. "Trust us."

I looked at Felix and Sam, not sure what to do. The secret recipe could burn my throat or make me gag. I might even double over and barf. Then again, it could get rid of my hiccups once and for all. I decided to go for it.

Taking the cup, I put it to my lips and drew the liquid through the paper towel. I nearly gagged, but out of surprise, not because of the taste. It was water. That's it. Cool, refreshing water. As I finished it off, Felix and Sam smiled at me. I took a deep breath and paused, waiting for the trick. But there wasn't one. With Felix on one side and Sam on the other, I put my arms on their shoulders. My hiccups were really gone. And my two best friends were back.